Quiet Money

**Lock Down Publications and Ca$h
Presents**
Quiet Money
A Novel by *Trai'Quan*

Lock Down Publications
P.O. Box 870494
Mesquite, Tx 75187

First Edition March 2020
Printed in the United States of America

Lock Down Publications
Like our page on Facebook: Lock Down Publications
@
www.facebook.com/lockdownpublications.ldp
Cover design and layout by: **Dynasty Cover Me**
Book interior design by: **Shawn Walker**
Edited by: **Shawn Walker**

Stay Connected with Us!

Text **LOCKDOWN** to 22828 to stay up-to-date with new releases, sneak peaks, contests and more…

Thank you!

Submission Guideline.

Submit the first three chapters of your completed manuscript to ldpsubmissions@gmail.com, subject line: Your book's title. The manuscript must be in a .doc file and sent as an attachment. Document should be in Times New Roman, double spaced and in size 12 font. Also, provide your synopsis and full contact information. If sending multiple submissions, they must each be in a separate email.

Have a story but no way to send it electronically? You can still submit to LDP/Ca$h Presents. Send in the first three chapters, written or typed, of your completed manuscript to:

LDP: Submissions Dept
P.O. Box 870494
Mesquite, Tx 75187

DO NOT send original manuscript. Must be a duplicate.

Provide your synopsis and a cover letter containing your full contact information.

Thanks for considering LDP and Ca$h Presents.

PROLOGUE

It was once considered a loose alliance of criminal elements that were structured and governed by a strict code of silence. It had enacted a campaign of near utter lawlessness and extreme violence in Sicily, around the 15th century. Its members were often tied together by a blood oath and sworn to secrecy.

The Mafia was first constructed inside of Italy's Sicily, in order to build a defense to protect the lands and property of the Land Lords, who weren't always present. However, by the 19th century, the structure had become a network of criminals who had come together to overthrow the Sicilian country side. Its members were bound together by what was called 'OMERTA', a strict, unbreakable code of conduct, which advocated avoiding all contact and cooperation with the authorities. The Mafia didn't have a central organized structure. It consisted of many small groups which were autonomous within their own area.

Sometime in the 19th century, members of the Mafia immigrated to the United States and were soon knee deep in American Organized Crime. A lot of Americans stepped into the media, at times, to down play the power and influence of the Mafia. Some had even gone as far as to deny the existence of a Black Mafia completely, but, Black is not a color, it's a reality.

ANOTHER TRAI'QUAN ORIGINAL…

CHAPTER ONE

To my Diary:

Dear Diary, I know that it seems as if I've been taking some time off. Especially when it doesn't seem like I have the time to take, but that isn't my issue at the moment. Lately, I've been thinking about my youth. When I was around the age of twelve or so, my brother was murdered in front of me. I really think that it caused some serious psychological and emotional issues with me. It was also along this same time that my belief system crashed. I simply refused to believe a God that was all good would allow an innocent child to be murdered right there in front of me. I was convinced that it happened in order to wake me out of my slumber and bring me to a certain reality. Thus, as time would pass, I came to resent most things. I burned my birth certificate when I was fifteen, as a show of my independence. I refused to be a conscious American, I was just a man. I also came to realize that I was a man who craved power. So, I told myself that one day, in my near future, I would come into this power and I would use it, the best way I could, to show that I was never weak.

You see, I had a chance to save my brother, but I didn't because I was afraid. It was that fear that motivated me to never accept weakness as an only reality.

****

JANUARY 2008
Q

The house he pulled up to was located out in Martinez, Ga, in an area where one wouldn't catch too many black people hanging out. Some called it Klan country, while others just kept the hell away from it.

The house itself looked large. There was even a carport on the side, along with the well-manicured lawn that was verdant and bright green. This community, he knew, consisted of the so-called wealthy. Doctors, judges, expensive high-profile lawyers and other law makers in and around the City of Richmond County. Actually, Augusta was the city. Nevertheless, out there it was about thirty percent whites and seventeen percent mixed, successful others. You couldn't really say blacks, because those blacks who lived out there wouldn't check off *Black* on an application.

He pulled the 2006 Camaro into the driveway and eventually parked next to a blue 7Series BMW 745i. He could see the tail lights of the Lexus LS-400 that was parked in front of him. There was an S-500 Benz sitting next to it and all the time he was thinking about how he was driving this rental car.

Either way, he reached over to the passenger seat to retrieve the leather-bound attaché case and turned to exit the car. He was just about to step onto the patio when sounds of the dog barking grabbed his attention. Aptitude caused him to glance around, even though he knew for a fact the dog was on a chain in the back yard. It was the fact that he held such a strong dislike for dogs.

Man's best friend? Yeah right, he thought. He made his way to the door where, he rang the bell.

The door was opened a few seconds later by a young, white girl with light blond hair. She wore an AC/DC t-shirt and ripped, denim jeans. With an attitude that said *don't socialize with the help,* she turned and left him standing in the doorway by himself.

He wasn't surprised, the bitch acted like Bill Gates was her old man. Either way, he stepped inside and close the door behind him. It was a good thing that he already knew how to find the study, because he wasn't about to call that punk ass bitch back and ask her shit. He wasn't one of those niggaz who had Martin Luther King Jr's. dreams. He walked down the hall thinking, *That may be the reason the bitch acted stuck up. That or she was racist.*

When he reached the door that led into the study he stopped. He raised his hand to knock but before he could, he heard a voice on the other side.

"Yes, come in," the voice beyond the door called out.

Since he knew the man was already expecting him, he opened the door and stepped into the small business style office. The inside consisted of a desk with one chair behind it and one in front of it. There was a Dell computer on top of the desk, a filing cabinet to its left and a mini sofa sat along the back wall. Seated behind the desk was an elderly looking white man, who looked like he was somewhere around sixty.

"Ah, Merrick. How are you, my friend?" The man asked and then waved his hand towards the seat. "I would offer you a drink, but we're not in the den area and I don't drink in my office," he explained.

Merrick took a seat across from him, in the chair that faced the desk and sat the briefcase on the floor. This was business, there was nothing at all personal about the meeting.

"Well then," the old, white man's eyes fell to the brief-case and then looked back to Merrick's face, "how have you been?"

"Look, Mr. Wilson…" Merrick started, but was cut off.

"Brad. How many times do I have to tell you? We've been doing this long enough, wouldn't you agree?" he asked.

Although he really didn't see the point in all of this fake friendliness, he still corrected himself. "Okay then, Brad, listen, I would really like to make this delivery and be on my way. I have some things that I need to attend to," he explained, but that was only partly true. He really didn't want to be in this house any longer than he had to be.

There was a moment of silence and then Bradly Wilson nodded. "Very well."

Merrick lifted the briefcase and passed it across the desk. The white man received it, placed it on top of the desk in front of the computer and then he opened it. Inside, there were stacks of fresh bills, which all looked like they were of large denominations. Both men knew from past experience that there were only hundred-dollar bills on top.

Back in the late 60s and early 70s, the Federal Reserve Bank had stopped issuing any bills higher than the $100 bill. Every time someone used anything larger, the bank would remove it from circulation as soon as they were able to get their hands on it. To see any bill larger than a $100 bill said one thing, *old money*. Not too many people could even tell that the face on the $500 bill belonged to William McKinley.

Merrick saw a smile creep onto the white man's face when he began to remove the bills on top. A smile of greed.

He placed three stacks of $100 bills in front of him. "That is the usual, right?" Bradly Wilson asked.

Overlooking the fact that it was supposed to be more, Merrick looked hard into the other man's eyes. He wondered if Bradly's clear blue eyes could detect the emotion behind his grey-green eyes.

"It'll do," was all he could say without showing his emotions.

****

Merrick closed the door behind him as he entered the apartment, exhausted from the past two nights. He hadn't been to sleep in over seventy-two hours because of all the driving he had to do. He went straight upstairs to his room and didn't even realize that he was that tired until he fell back onto the bed. The reality hit him and he didn't even feel like getting up to take a shower.

As the exhaustion set in and his eyelids began to feel heavy, his mind drifted. When he first got into this game, he explained to Bradly Wilson that he wasn't about to sell drugs. He wasn't anyone's bitch and he wasn't about to get pimped like one. Wilson explained it all to him, or rather, enough to understand that he wasn't involved in drugs, he was just delivering money. On top of everything, he was doing it for the Chief Investigator of the Richmond County Sheriff's Department. He didn't think he could get into that much trouble.

That was almost a year ago and now he knew a little more about what they were doing. The Federal Reserve was moving money from one location to another. There was a total of twelve Federal Reserve District Banks: Boston, New York, Philadelphia, Cleveland, Richmond, Atlanta, Chicago, St. Louis, Minneapolis, Kansas City, Dallas and San Francisco.

Since they were removing all five hundred, thousand dollar bills, other large notes and any old bills that needed to be replaced from circulation, they were stock piling it all before moving it. Each of the twelve banks had to collect the money from their region and when the amount reached a certain weight, it would be transferred to another location. At that location, the money would be documented and then burned.

Somehow Bradly Wilson had an inside source. All Merrick had to do was drive to whatever location, pick up some bags and take them to a warehouse. The person meeting him to receive the bags would in turn give him a briefcase which he would then take back to Wilson, who in turn would give him $3,000 for the drive.

Merrick had only done the drive three times. Tonight, was the fourth and because of how spaced out each job was, he wasn't able to save up any real money. These jobs were every three months and from one job to the next, he had to live like it was from check to check. However, when he had money to save, he made it a point to save it. He was good at saving money from his job and his hustles. Thus, he had a nice stash nested away. He was also saving to buy a ride when the time was right, but only time would tell if those plans would bear fruit.

****

I broke bread wit you nigga, showed you where I live, you talk it nigga but you don't understand what real is, when it came to you pussy ass nigga I would've killed, but it was my fault nigga I kept it too real!

The Plies ringtone shook him out of his sleep. He had to roll over twice before he found his LG, which must've fallen out of his pocket, it was lying on the floor next to the bed.

"Yooo," he spoke.

"Snipes, what up?" His partner Ameed asked.

They called him Snipes because someone said he resembled Wesley Snipes. Except for the fact that he was about three shades lighter and had grey-green eyes with a slight touch of brown in them. He did had a nice build, though, standing at 6'2" and a half, weighing 196 lbs, he was chiseled to perfection.

"Damn, bruh, what's da B-I?"

And before Ameed could answer, his moms happened to stick her head into his room. "Yo. Hold up," he said to Ameed. "What up, Ma?" He looked up at his mother. A woman who was homely, but still cute in her old age, especially after giving birth to two children.

"I need to know if you're still going to help with the bills. I want to get that out of the way as soon as possible."

Damn, he thought. He'd been so tired when he got in last night that he hadn't left the money out for her. "Is Jen gone already?"

"No, I'm going to drop her off myself," she replied.

That's when he checked the time on his phone and saw that it was still early.

"Alright, hold up." He clutched the phone between his ear and shoulder. Then leaned to the side and dug into his pocket. Ameed said something as he brought the money out. "What was that?" he asked while counting the money out.

"I said, this party later on got both of our names on it. So, what you wanna do?" Ameed asked.

He counted out $500, handed it to his mom and then pulled off another $200. "Yo, this is for the bills. Five is for you and give the other two to Jen, a'ight," he instructed.

She shook her head as she held the money in her hand. "Boy, I don't see why you give yo sister so much money. She ain't but fifteen, what she gone do with it?"

"Shoot, keep them lil flexin' ass niggaz out her face. This way she ain't gotta have envy reflecting in her eyes. I'd hate to have to mess one of these young niggaz around here up," he explained.

Both he and his sister had their father's eyes. His were mixed with both brown and green, while hers were green and grey. Their father carried the grey and green eye color.

"Well, at least she ain't like these other thots out here." She started to turn around. "Are you staying in today or not?"

"Nah, I've got something to look into."

He waited until she turned and walked out of the room before he spoke into the phone again. "So, what time and where?"

"Shiit, Patrice told me to meet her there around 9:30 or 10, but it's at her girl, Shaquita's apartment."

Patrice was Ameed's girl; they'd been together a few years, and she was like a little sister to Merrick. In addition, she possessed the ability to maneuver her way into a lot of their business, but she didn't move with aggression. She was pretty much family to them, and very much trusted.

Merrick was still stretched out across the bed, tired from the previous night when he remembered that it was still early and he had something to do when he got up.

"Look," he sighed. "I'ma pull up on you some time around 8:00 in the p.m. Right about now I'm still faded and I've gotta see this nigga, Andre, around 2:00."

"So, you decided to cop that whip?" Ameed asked.

Andre was the flip man. He made so much money flipping hot rides that he didn't have to do anything else.

"Yeah. In fact, I'm about to text this nigga now. Yo, I'll get up," he said and then ended the call.

He set his phone to wake him at 12:30 then fell back to sleep.

16

CHAPTER TWO

"Wait a minute. So, what you're telling me is that you trust this fuckin' mutt?"

"Listen Vincent, this is my guy. The motherfucker moves the way I tell him to move. I say breath and he ask how hard. So yeah, I trust him," Bradly explained.

He looked into the face of the Italian gentleman that sat across from him. Vincent *Vinny* Mendoza must've been around 56 years of age but could have been a year or two older. He was very distinguished and a damn good dresser too.

Bradly admired the $3500 Versace, two-piece suit and them $800 Mauri Gator dress shoes. Even the Cartier watch looked like it cost at least a grand. After ordering a bottle of Krug Clos D'Ambonnay 1996, which cost every bit of $2,195, he sat there thinking. Vinnie, like the other Italians from Elizabeth, N.J, didn't trust blacks.

Vinnie stubbed out the $30 cigar he'd been clutching between his lips, then glanced around the restaurant at the other people around them. He liked this type of crowd. Usually when he came way down here to the South, Bradly would set up a meeting at some God forsaken hell-hole that looked like it had rats. But this time he had earned Vinnie's respect. He'd actually picked a spot that reflected the truth of what Vinnie really was.

"Let me explain something to you Brad," the Italian said as he lowered his voice and held eye contact. "I don't like doing business with no moolies, I refuse to believe that they can be trusted. All of the sons of bitches are born two ways: fuckin stupid and greedy. But it's okay, you trust him and so you're responsible for him. Let's just hope he continues to be

Trai'Quan

trustworthy to you, because I'd hate for us to become enemies. That would be bad, very bad, Bradly."

Bradly didn't question just how bad it would be, but he hadn't seen anything flakey in Merrick's character yet. He knew the bags were unopened, they were sealed with those plastic zip locks, which made it nearly impossible to peep inside. Bradly was guessing that Vinnie was a little shook up because they had a big deal coming up soon and it was up to Bradly to get the shipment from point A to point B, without any problems. Bradly couldn't exactly make that happen without Merrick. So, he had to back him, black or not, it was all that he could do.

****

"Pussy ass cracker, give a nigga a hundred years, have yo mama leavin out the court room in tearz, crackers don't love the air a nigga breath for real, take a nigga life from 'em they don't know how it feel..." –Plies, 100 years

Merrick pushed the CD into the Sony changer as he sat in the driver's seat of the truck. Having just paid Andre for the truck and all of its accessories, he hadn't even pulled completely out of the parking lot yet and he had the $4,000 system blasting. Although the Cadillac Escalade Ext wasn't the next year's model, it was a 2006. The truck was still worth every cent he had spent. Especially with the Ashanti rims, 24 inches and pure chrome, encased in black to bring out their shine.

Merrick had been saving up for quite some time to buy the truck. At 19 years of age, he hadn't thought he would have his own. Not without standing out on a street corner and hustling crack, but he'd done it and kept his integrity. He hadn't sold the poison in the hood like other niggaz. The only thing was, he didn't exactly know how long this hustle would be good.

He put the truck in gear and signaled to turn out into traffic. Yeah, he needed to start thinking about a more solid position in his life. Which meant that he could either get a hustle, or get a better job. Right now, the 9 to 5 he had was moving slowly.

He whipped the off grey truck through traffic as he thought about it. The streets weren't where he was trying to be and even though he had graduated from high school, now days you had to have some college education just to get a three-star fast food job. He had none, which meant that if he wasn't gonna swallow that black pride shit and get knee deep into the streets, then he needed to think about starting his own business. But the thing was, what could he do? Every 4th nigga was trying to be a rapper and wasn't no Lebron James walking in his shoes. He didn't even know how to dribble a ball. So, what was he gonna do?

****

Ameed was Muslim by birth, but not by practice. He had respect for the religion because it was his parent's belief, but he just had too much going on. At 18, he was trying to get a grip on his life, while at the same time his little part time job at Chedder's up on Walton Way, wasn't talking about much.

The fucked up part was, although his moms had pulled some strings to get him the job, they were still bucking on giving him full time status. Nevertheless, he had his little side hustle. Ameed had the streets hot with that Osama Bin Laden, the best weed around. He had it because of his Jamaican connection.

He knew this nigga who worked with him in the dish room. The nigga had a cousin that was fucking with him. At the moment, he was moving a half pound, which had actually been more than usual, but he was still trying to stay below the radar. He wasn't trying to catch a Fed case.

****

"Damn, nigga, I like this bitch," Ameed said as he slid into the passenger seat of the Escalade.

"Shittt! Somebody had better like this muthafucka after I done spent all my money to get it," Merrick stated.

Once again, he pulled out into the streets. He lived in George Town with his moms and little sister and had to drive all the way to Harrisburg to pick Ameed up.

"So, look, I've got this blunt." Ameed held the apple flavor blunt up. Which had been gutted earlier and packed with some of his best bud. "We gone smoke or what?"

Merrick glanced over at the blunt. "The fuck you think? Nigga, light that shit." Then he pressed number four on his CD changer and his smoking blunts theme song kicked in.

Fire it up, fire it up... I grab the forty spark up the blunt, guzzle it, grab the mic and come out the woodworks, the situation leaves me no time to think, Keith Murry gets busy for basic instincts...—Keith Murry—Get lifted.

"Ayo, I just hope these dumb ass OS niggaz ain't at this party tonight," Merrick stated. He'd been beefing with them niggaz since he broke up with Tasha.

Ameed lit the blunt and hit it a few times. He coughed on the second long toke and then he passed it.

"Yo, nigga, you worry too much," Ameed told him.

"Call it what you want, but we—we both know her li'l brother got them GD niggaz on the bullshit." He passed the blunt back.

Neither one of them were in a gang, but with there being so much gang activity in the city at the present time, the police would show up as soon as they got a call. This situation between Tasha's little brother, Ant-G and him, was crazy. He'd always been cool with the li'l nigga, but when he and Tasha broke up last year, the li'l nigga began to get on the bullshit. Merrick had beaten the li'l nigga up twice already.

"Man, you know what? Fuck them niggaz," Ameed responded. "Let's just enjoy my girl's party and not look for trouble. A'ight?"

Yeah, A'ight, Merrick thought as he hit the blunt again. As if Ameed's temper wasn't worse than his.

They reached the party sometime after 10:00 and since it was being held in the Hell Street Apartments, the parking lot was full of different types of rides and people walking around drinking and smoking. Somehow Merrick found a couple of empty parking spaces. He parked, armed the Escalade's alarm system and then they both went to the heart of the party.

Just before they stepped inside, Ameed pulled out another blunt and sniffed it. He licked it, then he lit it. They walked inside, passing the blunt and choking together, but they polished it off in no time. They didn't even realize that they had posted up on the wall not far from the door. That was how good the weed really was.

"Ayo, sun," Ameed said, as he looked down at the roach that he held pinched between two fingers. "I'm about to go find a drink, what up?"

"Belvedere and Grey Goose. Just one cup," Merrick said.

Since he was the one driving, he wasn't about to drink a whole lot, especially knowing he'd just gotten the truck. Ameed had stepped off to get the drinks and Merrick stood there glancing around. It seemed to be an alright crowd, usually, niggaz would be trying to shoot up the place by 9:45. But then, Hell Street was damn close to 401 and even if the cops were using Phinizy Rd., the new jail, more, 401 was still the jail. Which meant, there were still cops at this bitch.

Merrick had been looking around, he really didn't know a whole lot of people down this way. This was more Ameed's scene, he was the one who did the hustling. Hustlers in Augusta were known and they knew everybody. The only dirt Merrick had accomplished that was known, was boosting cars for Andre. That was actually how he met Bradly Wilson in the first place, but his thoughts were interrupted by a vision of loveliness, dancing in the middle of the room.

The girl was pretty, even from a distance and in dim lighting. He watched as she did a two-step with a glass in one hand. She was wearing what looked like a Perry Ellis, form fitting dress and some two-inch Jimmy Choo heels. She was tall, too.

He would guess that without the heels she was six feet even. Yet her best feature was her skin complexion, the girl had to be the darkest person in the room, she was damn near blue black. The way the dress hugged her body, all 140 lbs. of it, made her 34-26-40 figure pop. Merrick was wondering why she was dancing by herself and then, as if he'd spoken her name, the girl turned and looked in his direction as she continued dancing.

The world is yours and everything in it, it's out there get on your grind and get it. Heyyy. Hands in the air, skies the

limit nigga, hands in the air—Jeezy's—Thug Motiva-
tion101.

She couldn't be looking at him, he thought. Yet when
Jeezy said, *hands in the air*, she raised her drink to the sky in
his direction and continued dancing. Then he became aware
of the guy standing next to her. He'd missed the nigga
because he'd been in a conversation with another nigga, but
as the girl kept dancing, he watched her, too.

Merrick could have sworn they had established some
type of eye contact, but that magic was broken when the DJ
changed the song on them. Now he was playing something
by Li'l Boosie called *Set It Off.* That was also the time when
Ameed returned and handed him a cup.

"Nigga, this party is off the chain," he stated. "But yo, I
just talked to Patrice. She said that she intended to introduce
you to her cousin, but she showed up with some other
nigga," Ameed explained.

"She still trying to hook me up? I thought she had better
things to do."

Merrick wasn't exactly shy around girls. It was just that
he wasn't into the whole relationship thing right now. Right
now, he preferred the slutty chicks who weren't into com-
mitments, especially after that thing with Tasha went bad. He
now knew that it had been a mistake from the jump. Then
out of the blue Patrice pushed through the crowd and stood
before them.

"What's up, Snipes? You enjoying the party?"

It was hard to believe that as short as this girl was, she
thought that she was a bully. Patrice was 5'4" and had sort of
a high-pitched voice. Body wise, she had large titties and a
nice ass, but it was her white girl titties that drew all the
attention, the damn things had to be a 38DD. Aside from

that, she was brown skinned and had long hair. Her and Snipes were more like brother-sister, than anything else.

"It's nice," he told her. "Better than what I expected."

Patrice said something to Ameed and then she laughed, but he wasn't paying her any attention. The dark-skinned girl held his focus once again and Patrice noticed.

"Oh, so that's what you like, huh?" she asked, drawing his attention. Then she too looked at the girl. "I don't know that girl, but the nigga she wit' is bad news. He's one of them Bloods from Sunset," she explained.

It was a wonder he hadn't realized the nigga was a Blood. He had on so much red that he looked like he was bleeding.

"Yeah, it might be best if you leave that one alone," Patrice said. Not that she thought he was scared, but because she already knew he was going through something with the GD's from O.S.

"So, I heard you trying to hook a nigga up," he stated.

"Yeah, but the bitch showed up with another nigga. So that ain't gone work, but don't sweat it I still got you, though," she said.

"Well, since I'm single, I'm about to get my flirt on. See if I can find me some loose pussy for the night."

All Patrice could do was shake her head.

Still sipping on the same drink, he moved through the crowd. The DJ was playing *I Got Dat* by Webbie, but he wasn't really into a lot of the Southern music. Some of it head potential, but both he and Ameed were from up North. Ameed was from New York, while he, his moms and sister, were originally from Camden, New Jersey. The move to the south came six years ago, when his mom realized that Camden was not a good place for his sister, Jennifer, to grow up.

The murder capital of New Jersey State, over half of the people in Camden were black. There were a lot of Latinos, too, but Camden's' median income per-household was something around $23,000 a year. There weren't any serious jobs and it was a wonder that they'd made it in the first place, which was in part due to his old man, who was now in Federal prison with a 20-year sentence for drugs. He'd been in for over 10 years. He was also the reason that Merrick wouldn't sell crack and he'd gotten educated by the New Jersey car thieves.

Merrick stepped outside where the party was even liver. Someone tried to hand him a blunt, but he declined. As a rule, he didn't smoke anything that anyone other than him or Ameed had rolled. Niggaz were putting too much shit in weed these days.

"Is that Seaside that you have on?"

He turned and looked around as if he'd just been caught doing something he had no business doing. His eyes came to focus on the dark-skinned girl from earlier. "Come again," he said, confused. The girl smiled and he saw that she also had dimples.

"The cologne you're wearing, it smells like Seaside Escape. I knew someone once who wore it," she explained.

As she spoke, it hit him that the girl had an exotic accent, one that he hadn't heard before.

"Yeah, that's how I'm doing it. Didn't I just see you inside with one of them Blood niggas?"

"That's my, so-called, boyfriend, Sleepy," she told him.

CHAPTER THREE

He had a cigarette behind his ear so he removed it and pulled out his lighter. The girl stood there and watched his movements. "My name's Merrick, but niggaz call me Snipes," he said.

"I'm Kenya," she smiled.

"So, where you from?" Merrick asked.

"They call it Cherry Tree Crossing, but it used to be called Sunset."

"Yeah, I know about the Set, but that wasn't what I was talking about. I was asking because of your accent."

Kenya smiled, showing her dimples. "Oh, I'm Puerto Rican."

"Puerto Rican and Black?"

"No, Puerto Rican," she explained. "Contrary to popular belief, all Puerto Ricans are not light-skinned. A great portion of us who come directly from the Caribbean Islands, are dark-skinned people and the majority of Caribbean people speak Spanish. But most Afro-Caribbean people speak Creole or Patois."

He knew some of that from the Latinos who lived in Camden, but not the history of it being mostly black people. He'd never seen one that was as dark as she was. He was just about to tell her this when he saw Patrice come running out the door.

When she saw him with Kenya her face twisted up. "Snipes, Ameed is about to fight two niggaz," she announced, damn near out of breath.

"Shit!" Cursed Merrick. He tossed the Newport to the ground and didn't even excuse himself. Instead, he stepped around the girl and followed Patrice back into the apartment.

Once inside, he saw that a crowd had gathered but Patrice pushed through it and he followed right behind her. As they made their way through, he saw Ameed standing toe to toe with two Sunset niggaz.

"Listen, since you niggaz don't know how to act civilized up in my girl's spot, how about y'all leave? Let the other people who don't want no problems, enjoy themselves," Ameed said.

"Nah, nigga," one of them said, shaking his head, "that's a negative. You can't put me out."

He was an average height nigga, with a somewhat chunky build. It looked like he might work out a little. While the other one just happened to be the one Merrick had seen with Kenya earlier, the *so-called* boyfriend. But he was being quiet, just watching his man's back.

"Look, nigga, I really don't want to fuck up my *Maurice Malone* shirt fuckin' wit' you." Ameed looked the nigga up and down."

Everyone watched as the look on the dark-skinned guy's face changed. "I tell you what," he stuttered. "Nigga, let's take it outside, one on one. Just you and me."

Merrick watched as Ameed sized the nigga up again. "You sure? You might need just a little bit of help, I mean, since you drunk and all."

"Pussy ass nigga! Sunset niggaz don't do no flexin," he said.

Ameed sighed. "A'ight, since you running your mouth, let's do this. I'll be outside."

The room thundered in oohs and aaahs. Ameed turned and walked towards the door as he acknowledged Merrick with a slight smile. Everyone that was inside, poured outside to the parking lot right behind him. A circle was formed by the crowd, with Ameed and the dark-skinned nigga in the middle.

Merrick had his eyes on the other one, Kenya's boyfriend, who stood on the edge of the circle. He also noticed that J.T. and Hightower were in the crowd. Both of them were from Broad Street and bought their weed from Ameed. He also knew that they had a rep for giving out the most beat downs by a two-man team. They were always fighting somebody.

"I've got a hundred on the dark-skinned nigga."

"Who said that?" Ameed asked, looking around until he saw the person with the hundred. "I'll take that bet. Anybody else like this nigga for a bill?"

But as he asked the question, it seemed that his cockiness changed the minds of a lot of people. "Look, pretty boy, you gone fight, or play with these chumps? Reminds me of them wolfing ass niggas who was at Hancock State Prison, with me," the tough guy said.

"Hold up, bruh. Aye yo Snipes, hold my shit," Ameed said. He removed the 1/2-inch rope necklace and his Movado, then he removed his Maurice Malone shirt and handed it all to Merrick. That left him standing there in his black Timberlands, Parasuco jeans and a black Sean John tank top. Ameed took a moment to smile at Patrice, who wasn't worried because she had watched him and Merrick spar several times and seen Ameed fight, then he turned and said, "You ready, tough guy?" Ameed smiled. "Or do you wanna call back to the prison and tell niggaz you met Jesus?"

The nigga didn't answer, instead he began to bounce around as if he were in a boxing ring, about to fight Floyd Mayweather. Everyone watched as Ameed cracked his neck and then stretched his arms. It seemed like time stood still and every third person was holding their breath when the dark-skinned nigga crouched down like a bear about to rip a hole into a deer.

Ameed didn't feel like a deer, though. He didn't move anything but his arms. The first punch was a right hook that hung in the air. Ameed leaned back slightly and swatted it away like a fly. The next one was a straight jab, which hit Ameed in the chest. It almost looked like Ameed wasn't going to throw any offensive blows, all he did was block those that were being thrown at him.

Merrick, unlike the crowd, already knew what would eventually happen. He watched as Ameed blocked a nice three piece, then he stepped back and dropped his hands. "Listen, bruh, you can still save face and take the easy way out, it doesn't look like your fight game is all that official," Ameed told him.

"Ain't no way, I'ma let a pretty boy whup me. It ain't over yet, nigga," he said. "It ain't over."

"So, what you're saying is, you're really serious about this?" Ameed asked.

"Fuckin' right. Ain't nobody going nowhere until one of us is stretched out on this grass."

There were a few ooohs and aaahs. Merrick almost wished the nigga would've taken the choice and left. He also noticed that the friend was becoming jumpy over on the sideline.

Ameed switched his fight game up. They considered niggas from the South to be swagger jackers because they would see or hear something, take it for their own, try to put a twist on it and then call it something else. Ameed switched up to an old New York dance style. It was originally created in the 70's and 80's, they called it the *Disco*. As times changed and Kung Fu Matinee hit Brooklyn pretty hard, niggaz grafted Kung Fu moves into the Disco and re-named it *The Fifty-Two Hand Blocks.* Somebody in the South got hip to it around the late 80's and called it the Alto Shuffle, which New York niggaz thought was some bullshit because anyone who knew 52 hands could walk right through it.

Ameed switched up again, to a Flatbush style, mixed with a little Southpaw. A style he and Merrick developed together. The dark-skinned nigga threw a left hook that Ameed weaved. A short jab followed, punch for punch, combo for combo, but when the nigga squatted to launch an upper cut, that's when Ameed opened up. The first few jabs were set-ups. They stunned the nigga, but he didn't move. Ameed leaned in with an over hand, right hook. He expected the nigga to dodge it, which was why he made it noticeable and the nigga did, but Ameed had planned for it and come right back with an elbow that caught the nigga across the jaw.

That sent the nigga sideways. Ameed moved in like a predatory animal stalking its prey. The nigga threw his guards up to protect his face, but the attempt itself was futile, instead of looking for an opening, Ameed simply began to batter the nigga's forearms until he had no choice but to drop his arms. Upon which, Ameed unleashed a series of jabs and hooks that were designed to make the nigga submit. When he saw that the nigga was about to go out, he moved in real close, bent his knees slightly, twisted his body halfway, with his fist balled up and elbows tucked into his stomach. Ameed pushed up from his thighs and hit him with an upper cut that was followed by an upwards elbow. The nigga was literally out on his feet, but Ameed stepped back and watched him fall like a tree.

He didn't see the other guy move, but Merrick did. The other nigga started to step forward like he wanted to get involved, but Merrick spoke up. "Now see," he began as he started to unbutton his Prada shirt. He handed Ameed's things to Patrice, "that nigga was nice. Real nice in fact." He pulled his shirt off and handed it to her, too. "But my only critique is that he took too long."

The nigga, Sleepy, held eye contact with him. "What? You lookin' like it's my turn to have some fun." He rolled his head on his neck and looked like he was loosening up and getting ready to fight, but after a moment's pause, Sleepy ended up helping his partner get up. As they stood, he took one more look around. Then his eyes met J.T and Hightower. He watched as they both lifted their shirts, showed off their Glocks and shook their heads. Instead of making a bad decision. He turned and walked off, carrying his partner.

When everyone saw that it was over, they started back to the apartment. Merrick was about to follow, but when he turned, he nearly bumped into Kenya. She smiled and handed him a piece of paper. Before he could say anything, she stepped past him and walked in the same direction as the crowd.

CHAPTER FOUR

Real nigga status, that's what I got, it ain't hard to believe it,
uptown that's where that work at, you can get murked easy.
Leave me around these killers I don't feel safe around
busters, if they could they'll tell God on Jesus, good rattin
mutha fuckas----Souja Slim & BG—Thug Brothers.

He woke up to the sound of his sister and his mom argu-
ing about something. He listened for a moment and decided
that it wasn't serious, so he sat up with his legs over the edge
of the bed, rubbed his eyes and tried to get them to focus. He
pushed himself up and went to take a quick shower.

Merrick ended up standing under the spray of the water
for a long time while he was thinking. His thoughts were on
Bradly and his crooked ways. The fact that he was a crooked
cop didn't really bother him. There were a whole lot of
crooked cops in Camden, N.J., so he was used to them, but
Bradly had his hands into everything. He was also controlling the dope game with his snitches. That was the new
hustle for the police, they were making their snitches big
dope boys and these same snitches were helping the cops put
cases on other niggas. Then there was the thing with the
money. So far, he'd figured out that there had to be some
Federal people involved. The times that he had driven, they
had moved too much money if what was in those bags was
what he thought it was. Yet nobody caught on to it. For it to
stay under wraps like that, it meant some important people
were involved. But the question was who?

****

"Merrick, I have an order for you," Tammy called out.

"A'ight, I'm on it."

He took the carry out pouch, snatched up his Domino's pizza hat and headed out the door. The address was on a piece of paper that was attached to the receipt. He glanced at it when he made it to the delivery truck, 2160. He knew the street and even the area, but not the address itself.

Merrick had been working for Dominos a little over a year now. As far as jobs went, it wasn't as bad as some. He only had to work through the week, from Monday to Friday. Most of what he did was deliveries and clean up. He didn't cook anything and he rarely washed dishes. They had enough people to do all of that.

The address was on Tobacco Rd., so he turned on to the street and began looking for the place. 2140, 2150, 2160! The address was a small Law firm called Howard & Gibson Law at Law. The building wasn't all that big, it was only two stories with a fairly small parking lot. He found a spot to park and then grabbed the pizza and headed towards the door.

There was a desk that sat facing the door as soon as he walked inside. Behind it sat a beautiful brown-skinned woman.

"Yes, may I help you?" she asked.

"Uh, I hope so. Somebody named," he looked down at the paper. "Julius, ordered a pizza."

He stood there waiting while she reached for the phone on her desk. As he waited, Merrick glanced around. He saw some paintings on the wall, but before he could take in their perfection, she hung the phone up.

"Take the stairs. It's the office to your right," she explained. The way she spoke told him that she was one of those upper class, black people, who looked down on lower class black people, like him, but he didn't let it bother him.

He took the stairs up to the second level. Once there, he saw two doors, one read Marion and the one on the right said Julius. The lady down stairs must've assumed he couldn't read. He moved up to the door and knocked.

"Come in. It's open."

Merrick turned the knob and stepped inside. Sitting behind a desk was a well-dressed black man. The man was on the phone, but he waved Merrick forward. As he stepped forward, Merrick's eyes observed the things inside the office. He saw that the man had to be well over forty.

His conversation lasted a little longer, then it ended and the man looked up. "Is that my order?" he asked and reached into his pocket.

"Your name's Julius, right? Then it's your order."

"Alright. How much do I owe you?"

Merrick watched as the older man pulled out his wallet. Then he looked up waiting to hear the price. Merrick knew they'd told him the price when he ordered, but it seemed like he was waiting, as if something had changed. Merrick thought he knew what it was. "It's $14.90." He placed the pizza on top of the desk and pulled it out of its warmer.

The older man looked up at him strangely. The look wasn't the same as the one the woman down stairs had given him. His was more like being vexed, almost as if to say *Damn! An honest black man.*

"All I've got is a $20. Will that do for the cover and the tip?"

"It's good by me," Merrick told him.

"What's your name, son?" The lawyer asked.

"It's Merrick."

"Mmmh. Is that what they know you by at work?"

"Nearly everybody that knows me."

The older man paused, deep in his thoughts. "Well, my name is Julius and I have a feeling we'll be doing business in the near future."

Merrick didn't have a problem with that, but there was something that didn't make sense. "Uh, if you don't mind me asking, what made you send way down to the city to order? There's a Dominos and a Pizza Hut not far from here," he stated. "I mean, if you don't mind me asking."

"I guess you could say that I believe in doing business with my own kind. Those places you named, they're 95% white and white owned. Plus, their service is crap. I'm from the city myself, so I know where to go and eat my food in peace, without having a bunch of white people looking at me funny," he explained.

Merrick took a moment to think about what was being said in his ear. In more ways than one, he agreed. Whenever a black man got over that hump in the road and he didn't do it by selling drugs, white people really hated on him, but they did it in silence.

"But, as a lawyer, don't you defend whomever retains your services?" Merrick asked.

"To a certain degree. When I went in as part owner of this establishment, I didn't do so with the thought of political gain, greed and capitalism. No! My partner, Marion, and I are two of the six lawyers who work here and our main thing is blacks who can't really afford the legal assistance they truly require. Those blacks who have become victims of the political aspects of the law. Those who can't get equal justice," he explained.

"Look at you for instance. You work for white people, but you work in a predominantly black area. Unconsciously, you aid the whites who earn their expensive lifestyle off of the minority. But if you ever become a victim to their unjust, self-imposed legal system, those white business owners won't bail you out. Your job may pay $23,000 a year, but that's not even enough for a white defense lawyer to represent you. Especially if you've come home one night and found someone has raped or murdered your loved ones. At that point, you would become emotionally involved and you'd pick up that same gun that white America manufactured and set out to get your own justice." He paused a moment then continued. "Then who pays for your legal aid? The tax payers, with the Public Defenders who get you off the hook for forty grand. But since the state provides five grand and they have higher paying cases, they don't put the proper amount of time into a case like that. You would end up going to prison and they tell you they did the best that they could, all you have to do is appeal." Julius sat back in his chair. "No, we started this firm to help our own, in the event that we assist a few whites here and there. We think of it as being fair and non-bias."

Merrick didn't see any way he could argue or debate about what Julius had just said, he actually understood the whole thing.

****

"Merrick, you've been in a daze most of the day. Are you alright?" Tammy asked.

He looked over to where she sat in the passenger seat of his rental. Merrick had been giving her a ride from work because they were friends. Tammy was a nice-looking woman. She had a soft, brown skinned, complexion, with perfectly rounded eyes and short curly hair. When he first got the job at Dominos, he'd thought about getting with her, but as it turned out Tammy was super cool and reminded him of Jen.

"Just had some shit on my mind," he told her.

"Well, I don't know what it is, but I hope you figure it out before it stresses you out."

He pulled up to the curb next to the sidewalk that led up to her apartment and said, "Listen, boo, you're a good friend. If ever there's anything I can do for you, just ask and I've got you."

"Well, shit, since it's that easy, I've got problems with bills. My baby's daddy ain't taking care of the bedroom. So, I haven't had any good sex in about five weeks. I need a car, hell, how many problems I gotta have to get some real help?"

He laughed. "I don't know, but I'm tempted to help you out with the first two. Especially the sex."

"Nigga, you betta watch it before I sit that friendship to the side." She laughed too, got out and he pulled off. He knew his moms was at work and his sister wouldn't be home from school for about an hour. He had enough time to shower and then see what the streets were talking about.

****

As he was getting ready for a shower, he pulled every-thing out of his pockets to put his clothes in the laundry basket and found Kenya's phone number.

"Say, Snipes, I need $200." Jennifer stuck her head into his room.

She looked exactly like him, only a younger version. On top of all that, she was starting to develop a body. He just knew that he was gonna hate that shit.

"What you need $200 for, baby girl? It ain't shopping weekend yet."

Merrick had started the habit of giving both his mom and sister $500 after he made a trip. Money for them to go shopping with. He didn't want them hurting for anything so he provided it. They had all types of clothing that were name brand, from Baby Phat to Fendi. Shoes that were by Jimmy Choo, jewelry by Kenneth Cole and Swarovski watches.

"I need to pay my phone bill and there's an upcoming school trip to Spellman College for the girls. I really want to go on that trip," Jen expressed.

Merrick thought about it then said, "A'ight, I got you. Give me a minute." He had to get the money out of his stash spot, which was a small six-inch section of the wall under his bed. He'd dug it out himself to hide his money, but he didn't have a problem giving her the money she asked for. Jen was his heart.

****

He pulled up at Ameed's house a little later. He went inside where he was immediately told, "Nigga, close the door before you let all of the weed smoke get out!"

Merrick closed the door and stepped into the house. He accepted the blunt and took a deep pull off of it.

"Oh, it's a good thing you pulled up," Ameed said. "That girl, Patrice, wanted you to meet us over at her place. She's spending the night."

"You mean her cousin?" He'd really forgotten about Patrice's' cousin, he was thinking about calling Kenya, but still hadn't gotten around to doing it yet. "You know what? Let's go check on that nigga, Zoe."

****

"Damn, Zoe, get yo damn feet off my coffee table," Li'l Mama said, causing both Merrick and Ameed to laugh as Zoe moved his feet while giving her the mean mug.

"Girl, I don't know why you wait until I've got company over to start acting brand new," Zoe said.

Li'l Mama was on her way into the kitchen and all three of them were watching her carry that big ass, even though they wouldn't say it. At 5" even, light-skinned and 146 lbs., Li'l Mama had a 38-inch ass that was stupid nice and round. For a girl that was short, she looked like a midget with an ass on steroids.

"Nigga, Snipes and Ameed ain't no fuckin company and if I catch one of you niggas wit yo feet up on my shit, y'all might as well be ready to take it outside," she stated, causing all three of them to laugh.

They knew she wouldn't put them out for real. Li'l Mama was older than all three of them, which was surprising since she let Zoe put his bid in. She'd already had two little boys and Zoe gave her a daughter. She lived in River Glenn and let Zoe push his dope out of her apartment, as long as he broke her off on the check.

"So, check this out, Zoe," Merrick said. "I'm trying to put something together and it's going to be major, but it ain't gone be no drug deal. You game?"

"Shit, I get a check out of it?" Zoe asked.

"Bruh, if this shit goes like I want, a check ain't even the word for it, but it might involve some gun play," he explained. "And we gone be on the road. It'll take us at least two weeks to do it."

He waited as Zoe calculated how much money he would lose if he took a two-week trip. "Shit, it's gone have to be a nice check, cause every time I get a little something, wifey spending that shit up."

"Nigga?" Li'l Mama came back into the room. "Don't be putting that shit on me. I told yo ass a long time ago that you should just buy yo own shit. But, nah, you wanna keep buying packages from these lames."

Once again, they all laughed, except for Zoe. He was really in his feelings about her putting his business in the streets.

"Yo, ain't you got something to do besides ear hustling on grown folks?"

"Nigga, y'all ain't grown. Can't neither of you niggaz buy beer." She turned and walked out of the room.

"Like I was saying," Zoe continued. "Yeah, if it means a nigga can get some serious work. I'll get down."

"A'ight," Merrick said. "I'ma call you when we get ready to put in that work. Just be ready. The shit should be happening in a few more weeks."

He really wasn't into the drug game, but the more he thought about it, there might be a way for him to finance someone who was. He decided that someone should be Zoe. He liked Zoe and he fucked with Li'l Mama, too.

Quiet Money

CHAPTER FIVE

"You want me to drive to Miami, Florida?" Merrick asked. Bradly looked at him closely, he knew that on this job, Merrick would be taking a big risk. He wanted to be sure that he could depend on Merrick. "Exactly. And I'll need you to take a female with you. This job will be slightly different, but you can send the woman shopping or something, you just need her for the ride," Bradly explained.

A female? Damn, this was looking better to Merrick. He had called Kenya a few times and the way she put it, her and ole boy were on the rocks as far as the relationship went, but he had only spoken to her twice before. How was he going to ask her to ride to Florida with him?

"I might have a girl, but what exactly do you want me to do?" he asked seriously.

They were sitting inside of California Dreams, haven eaten a small meal, when Bradly dropped the job on him.

"You'll meet up with a team once you get there. The team will consist of yourself and two others. They'll explain what you're supposed to do when you meet up with them," Bradly said. "In short, you'll be bringing two to three bags back up here. You'll call me as soon as you reach Augusta and we'll go from there."

On the jobs he did before, he would always drive to Atlanta and the people would just give him the package. This time he was doing some actual work. "Look, Brad, I'll do the job, but you're going to have to break bread this time. You're asking me to put my face on the scene. So that calls for more."

"I understand," Bradly said. "If you can pull this off, I'll give you more."

"So, when is the job?"

"Two weeks from today, but you'll be in Miami for a week to do the job."

Merrick was thinking now. He would have just enough time to put Ameed up on the job. If everything went as planned, he would get paid from both ends.

****

Kenya didn't have a car of her own, she didn't even have her own apartment. Instead, she was living with her sister Unice, who had two kids by a big drug dealer, named Ready Black. Kenya was the little sister. She was only twenty-two and hadn't been in the States but three months. The only reason she'd ended up with Sleepy was because he worked for Ready Black. Their relationship really wasn't a relationship.

Out of the three months she'd been in the States, she could honestly say that Sleepy hadn't made it to first base. Mostly because she could tell that he wasn't built the way that she liked her men, but they didn't even have the same interest. He liked *Boyz in the Hood* and *Friday,* while her favorite movies were *Belly* and *Shottas.* He liked Li'l Wayne and Pastor Troy, while she liked Fat Joe and Jada Kiss. There was nothing in common.

So, when Merrick finally decided to call, she sort of felt like a little girl again. They'd stayed up talking that first night, until the sun came up the next day and the second night, they talked for two hours. They had so many things between them that they both liked.

Truth being told, she loved her older sister and the kids, but she was sick and tired of sitting around the apartment doing nothing. She wasn't hurting, because Ready Black made sure that she had things, but the things she wanted the most, he couldn't give.

Go shawty, it's yo birthday, we gone party like it's yo birthday, you know I don't give a fuck cause it's yo birthday!
She walked into the kitchen, snatched her phone off the table and then looked at the number. Kenya smiled when she saw that it was Merrick. "Hey," she answered.

"How you doing, love. You busy?"

"I'm bored. Why, what's on your mind?" She wanted to know because she had nothing going on.

"Well, I'm thinking about swinging through and picking you up. I sort of need somebody to talk to."

"Well, it's 9:00 now. Don't you have to work tomorrow?"

"Yeah, I do, but I don't think an hour or two will hurt me. So, what's up, you game?"

She was thinking about how she loved his New Jersey accent. It made her tingle in all the right places. "Give me twenty minutes. I'll call you back and tell you where to pick me up," she instructed and then ended the call.

Kenya went to her room, removed her boy shorts and pulled on a pair of Baby Phat khaki shorts with a matching top. She slipped her feet into a pair of pink and white Airmax and then text Merrick and told him she would be standing in front of the grocery store on 15th Street, across from Sunset.

****

Merrick swung through five minutes after he got the text and scooped her up.

"Damn, love, do you look like that every day?" he asked, causing her to blush.

"Anyway, so what's on your mind?" Kenya asked.

"Do you mind if we just ride around? I didn't really have anywhere to go. You know, ride and talk."

"Sure," she agreed.

At first, they were both quiet. He didn't even have the radio on because he had so many thoughts in his head.

"You know," he began. "I sort of feel like you're this good girl and I'm having a hard time finding words to express myself to you."

"It's really not as hard as you think," Kenya said. "All you've got to do is be yourself. Don't try to change who you are to please me, it's who you are that interests me."

He thought about that a moment. Merrick wasn't all that good at building relationships. He never had been. "I just don't want to scare you off with the real me. Shit, sometimes the real me, scares me," he tried to explain.

Kenya was quiet for a moment. She was looking for the words to convey her own thoughts. "I came to the States because of something bad that happened to me in Puerto Rico," she began. She was really feeling Merrick. For some reason she felt that there was a connection between them and she didn't think that she wanted to lose that connection.

Merrick didn't speak. Instead he kept his ears open, there was something he was looking for, but he just couldn't figure out what it was yet.

"Last year I was raped by a guy that I thought I could trust," she explained. "As a result, I became pregnant and for the entire time I fought with myself about keeping the child. At first, I wanted to get an abortion, but I didn't have the money to pay for it and a bootleg abortion on the Islands could kill you. So, I went to see some people who wanted a child, but couldn't have kids." She paused as he continued driving, thinking and listening. "I never knew the nature of the child. Boy or girl, I couldn't say. I never held the baby, nor looked upon it, all because I was afraid. Being raped by someone that I originally thought I trusted," she fell silent for a moment and looked out the windshield, "that destroyed something inside of me."

Kenya paused a moment as if contemplating her thoughts and the words she'd spoken. She couldn't actually explain it so that it made sense. But she felt something drawing her to Merrick. Something that propelled her to open up and be sincere with him, which was something she hadn't done before.

"I just need you to understand my reality before we take this trip together. Especially, if I have to take the chance on trusting you," she explained.

Merrick listened to her story and although he wasn't a woman and couldn't physically or psychologically understand being raped, he understood pain. He had these migraine headaches to prove it. His story didn't take as long as hers, but he told her anyway.

Merrick explained how his younger brother was murdered by a white man as he watched, not able to do anything to try and save him. He told her how the fear held him frozen, like ice. He explained to her about his embarrassment and shame, but not about the headaches. He never told anybody about those.

He hadn't even realized it, but he'd parked the Escalade inside of the Augusta Malls' parking lot. Far away from any other cars that were out there.

"I need to ask you something," he stated. "I do more than work at Dominos. I've got this side hustle, but it's not pushing crack. I personally wouldn't touch that shit. However, there's this thing coming up in a couple of weeks where I'll need to be in Miami for a week." He stopped speaking and looked over into her face. "I know we've just met and while I would love to explore your deeper reality, this isn't about sex. I need a woman to ride with me. I'll make your stay for the weekend as pleasant as possible. You'll be able to shop, spend time on the beach, whatever."

He watched as her eyes searched his for something. Merrick didn't know why, but he sat still and didn't move.

"I'll go with you," Kenya stated. "If only to get to know more about you, but I'll ride with you."

When Kenya said ride, she literally meant *ride* with him.

CHAPTER SIX

I jog in the grave yard, spar in the same ring, now it's housed by the building where Malcolm X was slain, I spring train in the winter, round early December, run suicide drills over and over, with the weight of the world on my shoulders... Jay-Z—Lyrical Exercise

The music blasted out of the boom box, filling the back yard with the rapper's voice, while they worked out on the weights.

"Come on, you've got one more in you," Ameed called out as he stood over Merrick, spotting him.

At the moment, Merrick was down on the bench pushing the weights up off his chest and sure enough, he had three more in him. He sat up on the bench breathing hard. They'd been going at it for close to two hours now, trying to make up time because they both missed the last weekend, but that was the last set. Merrick reached for his vitamin water and turned it up.

"You thought about that thing I hit you with?"

Ameed was wiping the sweat from his body with a towel. "I mean, what's to think about? I follow you and ole girl down there, watch from a distance, peep the play and make a move. You said these bags weigh about 38lbs, right?"

"Yeah. One time on a trip to Atlanta, I had to carry two of the bags, but I'd say there was a little less than that, 50 lbs. Dumbbell..."

They both looked at the said weight. Merrick's weight set wasn't one of those cheap plastic ones. He'd spent every bit of three grand on it. So, his weights were the same as those you'd see in a professional gym.

"Yeah, I can grab two of those," Ameed said.

"But you're going to have to do it without being seen. That's the real issue," Merrick explained.

Due to the fact that he basically knew what the job consisted of, he had given Ameed the run down as best he could, without seeing the building.

"You know, this would be a lot easier if we pulled Zoe in on this," Ameed said. "I thought that's what you were going to do anyway."

"I was, but I thought it would be another Atlanta job. I didn't know they were sending me out of state and with another team too," Merrick said.

Usually all of the past jobs had been within the state of Georgia. It amazed him how good Bradly's inside people were. Everything always went the way he said it would go. He'd received his basic instructions about this job two days ago.

"So, I'll have to do this without back up," Ameed said. "Not that I'm shook bruh, but a plan B would be nice," he told Merrick.

"Actually," Merrick stated, "I've been thinking about something. I just haven't made my mind up about it yet. But don't worry about it, just focus on what I want you to do. The rest will fall into place."

****

"So, what you're saying is, you're going to Miami with this nigga for a whole week and you haven't even known him two months?" Unice questioned her baby sister as Kenya sat there looking at her.

Kenya nodded. "Yeah, that sounds about right."

Unice said, "This is fucking stupid," in Spanish and then threw her hands up in the air. She knew the life her sister was living at the moment wasn't ideal. Ready Black gave her money, but it wasn't anything extravagant, or lavish and that nigga Sleepy wasn't serious about being with her. Unice was almost positive that he was one of those homo thug niggaz, but she couldn't prove it. How else could you explain him being with her sister but choosing to spend more time with his niggas, rather than being with Kenya?

Unice sighed. "Okay, you're a grown woman. I was only trying to protect you, knowing that you don't know very much about the States. If you feel like you really want to see what this nigga is about, then so be it," she said.

Unice knew about the situation in Puerto Rico and what had happened with her sister, so she knew that she'd been over protective of her since she'd been living with her. She could see that Kenya wasn't really feeling it, which was a sign for her that it was time to take a step back and let her live.

****

"Oh, so Merrick is taking that girl with him, but you're not even asking me to go with you?" Patrice stated the facts to Ameed.

"No, see you've got it all wrong," Ameed tried to explain it to her. "This is not a vacation trip, it's about business. The people Snipes works for told him to take a female with him. She's like his cover. You know, like what secret agents do."

Patrice thought it over. She knew that Merrick had something else going on besides working at Dominos, but she didn't know exactly what. It wasn't selling crack that much she did know. Merrick wouldn't even ride in the same car with Zoe if he thought Zoe had some crack on him.

"And you're supposed to follow them in another car? Then do whatever it is Merrick wants you to do? All by yourself, huh?" She summed it up.

"Yes." He let out a sigh of exasperation. Her distrust was wearing him out.

It was Thursday now and they were leaving in the morning. Merrick had given Ameed enough money for him to rent a Lexus LS400. He had said that an expensive car would draw less attention. Especially driving to Miami and back. He would have the guns in the car, so he didn't need to get pulled over.

"Well, you might as well pull your phone out and call Snipes. Tell him that I'm your cover this week," she said and then crossed her arms, giving him a crazy look. "Go ahead call him," she insisted.

Ameed sighed, but he could see that she wasn't going to let it go. Maybe if she heard it from his mouth, she'd let well enough be. He pulled his phone out and dialed Merrick's number.

"Peace, what up?" Merrick asked as the ringtone ended.

"Yo, look, wifey ain't got no understanding about us leaving in the morning without her. She thinks if you can have Kenya along, as your cover, she should be my cover." He waited as Merrick seemed to be thinking.

"Where she at?"

"Standing right here."

"Give her the phone."

Ameed handed the phone to her and listened. "What's up, Snipes?"

"He doesn't know you already strong armed me, do he?" Merrick asked.

"Nope. And?"

"A'ight. Give him the phone back and go pack yo shit. We leave at 6:00 in the morning."

Patrice handed the phone back then turned and went into the apartment.

"Man, I'm sho' glad you straightened that up," Ameed said.

"Oh, yeah? Look, I'm pulling out at 6:30 on the head. You and Li'l Sis betta be at the I-Hop by 6:00 or it's a wrap."

Ameed was struck stupid. He thought Merrick had told her that she couldn't come. "So, she can come?"

"Yeah, she good. Remember, 6:00 at the I-Hop. Be there." Merrick ended the call.

Ameed shook his head. He didn't know what type of power Patrice had, but she was good. The girl was damn good.

****

Merrick clicked back over to his conversation with Kenya. They'd been talking when Ameed called.

"I'm back," he said.

"One of your bitches?" Kenya asked jokingly.

"First of all, the word *bitch* isn't a part of my vocabulary, unless I'm stressing about a *bitch ass nigga*. And since it's rare that I get into my feelings that deeply, I seldom have to express my emotions through anger.

"Secondly, I don't cheat. In the event I decide I want to fuck more than one woman, I'm either not in a relationship or me and my girl both like the same girl, but it won't be no behind her back kinda shit. Little boys play little games," he told her. He was quiet for a second then he added, "And last, just so we're clear before this trip starts, you haven't asked to be my girl. Nor have you made any claim on me as your man. So, you don't have the right to be checking up on my call waiting. Are we clear on all of that?"

There was another moment of silence.

"Oh, we're clear," Kenya stated. "But just so *you* know, I wouldn't be going on this little trip if I didn't think we were going to be together. Two, I'm not one of these little, soft girls you might be used to. And three, don't make me fuck you up because of yo slick ass mouth," she sucked her teeth.

"Shiiit, it sounds like we might have a beautiful relationship," Merrick concluded. He intended to see if she was really built the way she just said she was. Because with him, a soft female wouldn't last long. A hard one, on the other hand, could definitely see a future with him. "You just have that ass ready when I swing through in the morning."

"Nigga, don't be sweating my ass." She giggled like a little girl. "We gone both be on point."

I hope so, Merrick thought. He was really hoping he wouldn't lose control. Nobody knew about his headaches, there were times when they were really bad. He just hoped he didn't experience any of the real bad ones in Miami.

CHAPTER SEVEN

I wake up wit' the birds when the nerds are asleep, I'm catching my second wind the second the first one ends. I am focused man and I'm not afraid of death...--Jay-Z— Lyrical Exercise

Vincent *Vinnie* Mendoza sat inside his study, looking at the fire burning in the fireplace. At the moment, he was thinking about The Mendoza's family history. He came from an old family, which wasn't straight Italian. Long ago, sometime after Benito Mussolini's' war against the mafia ended, after 1945, the Mendoza's, who were lower on the totem pole, came into play.

An ancestor of his was, at that time, a house boy. He performed various chores for the ruling family of that time. As time moved on, this ancestor developed a relationship with one of the daughters of the family.

In later years, they would marry and produce another male Mendoza. Their name, because it was a foreign family name, went unnoticed by the majority of the Italian elite. The mafia aristocracy would never have known that a bond servant, a serf, would one day rise from amongst them.

The Mendoza's would migrate to the States sometime around 1980, which was around the same time that Paul Castellano had his own butcher shop on Eighteenth Ave. in New York's Brooklyn Bensonhurst section. Castellano was actually seen as a bad boss, but was also respected as a business man. His greed turned a lot of people against him.

In December of 1985 Paul Castellano and his body guard Tommy Bilotti would eventually be murdered by, what most people assumed were the Gambino hit team. At this same point in time, unnoticed to the twenty-one captains of the

Gambino family, Mendoza was emerging as one of their street soldiers. He became a made-man and worked his way up through the ranks. From soldier he became a lieutenant and after a few successful jobs, he became a captain.

A few years later, when one of the bosses of one of the five families that lived in Bensonhurst had a problem, it would be Tony Mendoza who he would get to solve the problem. Tony, having recently married Pauline, who was a distant cousin to Carlos, whose sister was Kathy, which had been the wife of Paul Castellano. It was mostly the marriage that brought Tony to the boss's attention and with a brand-new baby, little Vinnie, Tony became an underboss because his blood wasn't pure or couldn't be traced back to the Gambino family. Tony could never rise above that position, however, he was treated and regarded as if he were one of the bosses.

Tony Mendoza passed away in 2003. But by that time Vinnie was already a captain in his army. So, when Tony passed, the position was offered to Vinnie. Even though no one expected Vinnie to turn in down, he did.

With Gotti in Federal prison because Sammy turned rat and so much internal conflict with the families, Vincent Mendoza continued to remained connected to the families. But Vincent no longer lived in Bensonhurst, instead he lived in Elizabeth, New Jersey, a city in northeastern New Jersey. It was the seat of Union County and it was a deep-water port in Newark Bay and Arthur Hill. It was also connected Goethals Bridge with Staten Island New York.

Elizabeth, New Jersey was also where those Mafia boss-es who ran, owned and worked the Casino's in Atlantic City, lived. So, when Vincent Mendoza came into contact with an FBI agent who got himself into debt at one of the Casino's and the agent, once pulled aside, told Vinnie about the

Federal Reserve, Vinnie paid his debt off in exchange for information. But he couldn't use the information in any of the states above Virginia, which meant that he had to bring in someone else and who better to bring in than his wife's greedy brother, Bradly Wilson.

The only thing that bothered him about the agreement, was that Bradly was using this nigger as a carrier and the one thing the FBI Agent had explained to him was that they couldn't get too greedy. They couldn't take so much that it would be impossible to write it off on the invoice. Since Bradly was sending the nigger to do this next job, he was worried that something would go wrong.

****

"This will actually work out for the good," Merrick said. He stopped eating his blueberry pancakes as he looked around the table. Kenya sat next to him and Patrice was across from her, with Ameed across from him. "The whole time we're down there, you and I can't be seen talking or even together, at all, which means that Kenya and Pat will be our only form of communication."

"Couldn't we just text back and forth?" Ameed suggested.

"Nah, because one, it's like leaving bread crumbs. What if these guys suspect me in the middle of texting a message and snatch it? And two, I don't intend on sneaking and doing anything. These people are some serious people. This isn't the dope game, bruh, this shit is federal."

Merrick had pretty much laid out what he was into, but he'd given Ameed more details since he needed Ameed to do the heavy work.

"So, that's all we get to do, deliver messages?" Patrice asked, with a questioning look on her face.

"Yeah, I wanna help, too," Kenya added.

While they all spoke at once, Ameed just shook his head. Merrick was the captain of the ship, so it was all on him. Every new call made, was his.

"I've been thinking about that, too," Merrick said. "When we get to Miami, I need you both to buy some all-black gear. Pat, I know you can shoot, but what about you, Kenya? Can you shoot a gun?"

Kenya bobbed her head. "I've shot a 9mm a few times. But nothing bigger."

"Wait a minute, bruh," Ameed said. "Are you seriously going to get them into this?"

Merrick gave it some careful thought. He'd been thinking about it all night and it made sense. "Look, you said we needed a plan B, because you would be going in alone, right?" Ameed nodded. "Well, what if they were your back up?"

They all sat quietly, thinking about it.

"You'll be the only one going in. But they can be on the outside watching out and covering your back. Since I'll be in there with their team, I won't be able to help. And they won't be in any real danger, they'll be on the outside."

"A'ight." Ameed stated. "We'll still have to wait until we get there. I have to see the lay out in order to put together my strategy."

Merrick finished eating then looked at his watch. It was about time and his head throbbed a bit. "A'ight. It's 6:20. Here." He reached into the inside of his Avirex U.S.A jacket and pulled out an envelope. "This is for you and Pat. It's ten grand. That should be enough to hold you for the week, we'll be staying at a Super 8 or a Comfort Inn. Make sure you pay for a whole week. Got it?"

****

Kenya really had the game fucked up. As tall as she was, standing at 6'0", when they stepped out of the I-HOP and walked to his Escalade, she looked like she was the same height as Merrick, being 6'2". But that was the three-inch Prada heels. It was the Seven jeans that made the meanest statement, Kenya was already dark skinned and tall, in those jeans he could see every aspect of the 40 inches of her ass. With her waist being small, she sort of looked like a coke bottle with a wider bottom. Her hair was spirally and not as dark as he originally thought it was.

"You wanna drive?" Merrick's head was about to hurt.

"Sure." Kenya accepted the keys.

As he went around to the passenger side, he saw that Ameed was also letting Pat drive the Lexus. Once inside the truck, Kenya started it and the CD player kicked in.

I know you have a little life in you yet/ I know you have a lot of strength left/ I know you have a little life in you yet/ I know you have a lot of strength left this woman's work, this woman's work... Maxwell

The CD that he'd been playing when he picked her up was still playing. Kenya pulled out of the I-HOP and into traffic. He'd already program the GPS with the best route to Miami, so she set cruise and followed that.

****

Ameed put his seat back and settled in to get some sleep. Pat had gotten her sleep last night, he hadn't because he had to stay up and clean all of the guns. Neither he nor Merrick liked using unsure guns so they made it a point to clean all of their guns before they used them. All four of the guns were Desert Eagle model and brand. There were two .44's and two 9mm's. All four guns held 16 round clips with the one round in the chamber. Ameed had broken each one down, cleaned them and then oiled them.

Merrick had been specific about the girls getting the two 9mm's, which meant the .44's would be used by them. That was, *if* they had to use them. But, from the way Merrick had explained it to him, it shouldn't be necessary for them to even pull the guns. That, he knew would be determined once he got a look at the building they would be going into. Either way, he figured that he would be able to devise a good plan.

****

They hit Jacksonville just before 12:00 and pulled into one of the truck stops. Although Pat parked right behind the Escalade, they didn't speak to one another because it was out in the open. No one knew if Bradly had someone following Merrick or not. To be careful, while both women went inside, Merrick and Ameed pretended to be having a casual conversation as two strangers pumping gas, so it didn't look out of place.

"You think they'll be able to handle the job?" Ameed asked.

"Well, Pat is from the hood, I'd imagine she could," Merrick said. "As for Kenya, I'm hoping she can, because if she fails this week…" he hunched his shoulders in an *I don't know what could happen* type of way.

"So, it's like a test on her end, huh?" Ameed asked.

"One that, if she doesn't pass, she won't be able to take over. But, look, how much weed can you get from your guy at one time?" He watched as Ameed thought about it.

"A few pounds, I've never asked for weight," Ameed told him. "Why you ask?"

"Because I refuse to sell crack to black people, but I will sell weed. So put your mind on it. Think about how we can build a greenhouse somewhere in Carolina. Maybe grow our own shit."

Ameed thought on it. "It might come out better if we get one of those RV's and have it gutted."

But before he could finish the thought, both the girls came back. This time they let Ameed lead since he wasn't driving the Lexus and Merrick was behind the wheel of the Escalade.

****

They reached Miami's City limits before 4:00 and not thirty minutes later, both of them were pulling into the parking lot of a Days Inn.

"Listen, when you pay for the room, get it for seven days flat and make sure they've got cable," Merrick told Kenya as he gave her a roll of money. There was two grand in the roll but he knew it wouldn't cost that much. He looked over and saw Ameed going inside with Pat. He pulled out a bottle of Advil and swallowed four of them. While they were doing that, he also pulled out his phone and looked up the number Bradly had him program in. He pressed send and waited while it rang.

"Yeah."

"Can I speak to Stuart?" Merrick asked.

"Who's calling?" The voice on the other end asked.

"Tell him Hannibal didn't invade Arabia and Czar only reigned in Rome." Merrick repeated the code then he waited. He could tell the phone had been muted, so he suspected the message was being given.

"This your number?" The voice asked.

"For this week it is," Merrick said. Bradly had told him to buy a burn out phone for the job.

"Where you staying?" The voice asked.

"The Days Inn on Fitzpatrick. I just checked in."

"What room?"

"Don't know yet. My wife's in the office now."

There was another muted silence, this one shorter. "Keep your phone on you and don't go too far. Stuart will contact you within the hour. Got it?"

"Yeah, yeah. Within the hour. Got it," Merrick said. The phone went dead and he looked up just as Kenya came back out.

"We're four rooms down from theirs," she said.

"Good. Come on, let's get inside," he said as he opened the back of the truck, pulled their bags out and followed her up to the second level where their rooms were located.

CHAPTER EIGHT

When the call came, Merrick was laying on the bed looking at an old episode of In Living Color, while Kenya took a shower. Before he answered, he pulled out the second pre-paid phone he had and text Ameed.

"Yeah," he answered.

"Go down to the parking lot. You'll see a black Range Rover parked near the dumpster. Get inside."

"What do I tell my wife?"

"Tell her you'll be out for about an hour or two."

"Alright. Give me a second."

He ended the call just as Kenya stepped out of the bathroom, but that wasn't what he held up for. He heard the two raps on the door then counted to ten. He got up and grabbed his .44, which he slid into his pants under his shirt.

"I'll be back in about two hours. There's some money on the bedside table. You and Pat can chill until we get back," he told her as he headed out the door.

In the parking lot, he didn't even look at Ameed as he got into the Lexus and began to back out slowly. Instead, he made his way over to the Range Rover where the door opened on the passenger side.

"Get in," a voice called out.

He pulled the door and hopped inside. No sooner had he sat down the truck started. Merrick looked at the driver, he was a big man, he couldn't tell how tall. He was damn sure built like he played for the Miami Dolphins. There was also another guy in the backseat. He too was big, like a football player. Both men looked like they were either Hispanic or Italian.

"You got a gun on you?" The one in back asked.

"Yeah," Merrick said as they rode.

"Take it out and place it on the dashboard where we can see it," the guy in the back said.

Merrick did exactly as he was told. Then waited.

"My name's Stuart, the guy driving is Ned. Not our real names, but the names we'll be using on this job. Your name will be Walt. Say it."

"My name is Walt," Merrick repeated.

"Good. Okay, just sit tight and let Ned do the driving. This part of the job is easy," Stuart said.

So, Merrick sat back and enjoyed the ride.

****

They ended up parked at Miami International Airport. Ned pulled up near the service area and parked the Range. He turned it off and sat there.

"You see that blue Lufthansa jet right there?" Stuart directed his attention to the jet and Merrick watched as the jet was being fueled.

"This is the job. Every Monday, Wednesday and Friday, that jet lands here, coming in from Frankfurt. On board there are bricks of $50 and $100 bills in bags. These shipments are coming in from a German bank and the average amount will be between 85 to 100 million per flight."

Merrick whistled as he heard the amount.

"This bank employs Brinks to move the bills. The Brinks people will move the bills from the tarmac to a warehouse over there. See the blue building with the large B on it?" He pointed far out to the airport's perimeter. "That's where customs officers go over them. The whole process takes about three hours." Stuart paused. "Here's what you don't see. Inside the warehouse, these bills will be laying out in the open, still inside the bags and all guards have to remove their guns before they enter the building."

"So, we're going to rob the joint," Merrick suggested.

"Not really," Stuart corrected. "The two of us work for Brinks already. On the day that we pull the job, we're usually short. On Wednesday, because it's in the middle of the week, there's only two guards, me and Ned. We're going to put Walt's name on the roster for Wednesday, as a temp-part time worker. That's only for the customs people's eyes, we'll have pulled some bags back so that when customs come, they'll go over those bags waiting to be moved. When they leave, you'll leave 30 minutes later in one of the airport vans with the bags inside. It's just that simple," he explained.

Merrick thought it over. He would need to let Ameed know that he would have to rob these guys. It would be the only way for this whole thing to go off without blowing up the whole hustle.

****

Ameed was parked a little further up the street. Using $1600 binoculars, he was able to see the Range and every-thing else. He could tell by the way the truck was parked, facing the blue warehouse, this was where the money would be. He observed it's every detail, the warehouse had large bay doors that led directly to the streets. From the looks of it, someone could bypass the perimeter fence and the airports' gate house, allowing them to gain access without being noticed. But he would have to talk to Merrick, he needed more information.

****

"What do you think about these?" Kenya held up a pair of black jeans and a black turtle neck.

"Probably make you look like a Black Panther." Pat said and they laughed but continued looking. They eventually found two outfits that were solid black and two pairs of black on black Timberland Men's Euro's. They paid for the items then found their way back to the Escalade.

"Damn, ladies, can the brothers get some attention?"

A group of guys called out as they walked by, but neither one of them took the time to acknowledge them. Instead, they had their minds focused on the job and they didn't even know the details yet. Never the less, they were taking it seriously.

****

Merrick returned to the room just after the two hours because they'd taken him to a second house where he picked up a brand-new Brinks security guard uniform. As he entered the room, he found Kenya sorting through the outfits she'd purchased.

"How you doing, ma?"

"I'm good." She looked up at him. "Is everything good?"

"Yeah, but we need to have a talk with Ameed and Pat." He hung the uniform up, then sat down on the bed and picked up the other pre-paid phone. He dialed Ameed's number.

"Ayo, peace!"

"What's up, bruh, where wifey at?" Merrick asked.

"She right here."

"A'ight. I need you to put your phone on speaker, everybody needs to hear."

"A'ight. Go ahead," Ameed said.

For the next hour, Merrick explained the situation to them. He listened to Ameed give his report then he told them how Stuart and Ned would pull some bags out of the official shipment. Ameed listened to everything that he said. When he finished talking, Ameed spoke again.

"Listen, bruh," Ameed said. "One of the girls gone have to go in with me. It's the only way this will work."

"What makes you say that?" Merrick asked.

"I mean, I could probably do it by myself, but it would implicate you. I would have to body both of them and even if I didn't, if I went in after you left, they'd swear you had doubled back and hit them."

Merrick thought about that and it made sense. He didn't want to bring any attention to himself what so ever. "A'ight. So, if you use one of them, who's the best choice for the job?" Merrick asked.

"Bruh, it would have to be yo Queen," Ameed said. "Look, Pat is too short and her titties are too big. We need to make it look like two guys rushed the spot. Kenya is tall enough and with a sports bra, it'll look like she's got a chest, not breasts."

"Yeah, but you are forgetting the damn girl has a big ass," Merrick said. "It's gone move and shake, bruh."

"Not really, she could buy some of those padded shorts they sell. The kind that are tight enough it stops movement. She wears those and some tight jeans and we good. Plus, we'll be wearing masks, all she has to do is not speak," Ameed told them.

The whole time, Merrick was looking into Kenya's eyes. She hadn't spoken a word yet and he couldn't tell a thing from the look on her face. He needed some more Advil. "So, what do you think, ma?"

"I can do it," she stated.

"Are you sure? I don't wanna put you in a tight situation if ya can't handle it," Merrick said.

The whole time his heart was fluttering like a whole lot of butterflies.

"Yeah, I can do it," she restated.

"Good," Ameed said. "Pat can drive the getaway car. Which also reminds me, we'll need to get a hotbox, too, that or a rental. You pick."

Merrick knew it wasn't about to be rented in one of their names but did he want to take the chance of Pat sitting in a hotbox, waiting on them if a cop comes by and runs the plates.

"I'll get the ride tomorrow. Don't worry about it," he told them. He had an idea.

****

Merrick couldn't even sleep that night. Tomorrow would be Saturday and they would have to wait three more days before they could pull the job.

He stood looking out the window, smoking a cigarette as he held a corner of the curtain back. There wasn't anything unusual going on outside and behind him, Kenya was asleep in the bed.

When she'd come out of the bathroom wearing the baby phat tank top and the boy shorts, he had wanted to get all up inside of her life. But he held himself back. This job was too important to him. He couldn't afford to have emotions involved at this point, which meant that sex would have to wait. Besides, after what she'd told him, he wanted to show her that it wasn't about all of that. If this was going to be *that* relationship.

Merrick wanted it to be that solid, he was thinking about the future and any future that would be his future, had to be governed by certain rules. He was still concerned about the migraine headaches; the Advil didn't seem to be doing much good lately. He might have to try something stronger.

CHAPTER NINE

Five in the morning, ain't nobody out but us, everybody sleep but we finna wake the city up, Finna teach you pussy niggaz bout playing wit 'us...— Goons Out Lurkin

One thing about being in a city, any city, big or small, a person could always find what they really needed in the hood.

It was Monday night and not only had Merrick found a used car that he was able to buy under a fictitious name, he'd also come across two bullet proof vests. Since he knew that he would be letting Kenya go in, he didn't even hesitate to buy them. Especially with Ameed stressing the *what if something goes wrong*, which was what he was doing.

Merrick sat on the bed watching TV with the phone lying next to him, on speaker. A bottle of Tylenol three sat on the bedside table next to him.

"Look, Snipes, I'm not calling bad luck down on us, I'm just trying to cover all of the bases. Plans like this can change at the drop of a dime, we both need to consider it and prepare for it," he suggested.

Kenya and Pat were out somewhere, they didn't make it a point to restrict them, instead, Merrick was the first to encourage Kenya to go out and have fun. Lately, they'd been doing a lot of talking but neither had made any attempt at sex. The mental connection was there so they were just going with the flow.

"Okay, so give me your worst-case scenario, if this should happen you do what?" Merrick asked.

"Okay, throw something at me," Ameed told him.

"If one of the two guys refuse to lay down?"

"I put one into him," Ameed replied.

"If one of them makes a country break?"

"I put a couple into him," Ameed said.

Merrick paused to think of something different. "If one of them ends up having a gun?"

"I put a whole lot into him."

"So, basically, if they act up, it's a reason for you to shoot somebody?" Merrick asked. He looked at the Tylenol Three.

Ameed was quiet a moment, thinking about it. "Yeah... Pretty much. See, now that wasn't so hard, wow was it?" Ameed asked.

Merrick shook his head. There was just no getting through to Ameed. If anybody did anything suspect, he was intending to body them. Headaches might be the least of his problems.

****

"How does this look?" Kenya asked as she turned sideways for Pat to look at her.

They were standing inside of a women's clothing store, where Kenya was wearing what looked like a girdle, which was specifically made for a woman's butt.

"It'll work. But you might have to get some jeans a size or two bigger," Pat told her. She watched as Kenya looked in the full-length mirror.

"Yeah bigger jeans should work," she said.

They later found some bigger black jeans and paid for everything so that they could leave.

"I really wouldn't mind coming down here to do some real shopping," Kenya said.

They were now walking towards the exit, having been in the mall for nearly two hours.

"It ain't like you can't come back," Pat told her.

"Please and spend whose money?" Kenya asked.

"Well, I thought you and Snipes were on the relationship level," Pat said.

"We're working on it. But even then, I'm not really into the gold-digging shit," Kenya stated. They'd stepped outside and were walking to the Escalade. Both had bags in their hands.

"You'll have some money of your own after the job. I know Snipes is going to look out," Pat told her. "Plus, you're actually putting in some work."

Once inside of the truck, Kenya started it and pulled out of the parking space. "Maybe it's because I've never really had all of this good stuff you women have," Kenya said. "When I see it, I want it. But to be honest, I don't think that I would really spend my money on it. I mean, it's just stuff and stuff comes and goes. It doesn't last forever."

There was silence as she drove, following the GPS as it showed her the way back to the Days Inn.

"So, tell me," Pat started. "If not for the luxuries or the chance to have some serious money to enjoy the luxuries, why are you even agreeing to put yourself at risk, doing this?"

Kenya drove a couple blocks, but was stopped at one of the lights that was red. "I'm doing it for the man," she explained. She turned her head and looked at Patrice. "I'm doing it because I want Merrick. But I don't want him like any of these other females out here, I want the realness of him." She fell silent as the light changed and she drove on. Her words still hanging in the air.

"All men are different. Each one brings something different to the table. As women, we choose our men by their advertisements. Be it the cars, jewelry, clothes, or the looks, the sway or their reputation, we look for those things that appeal to us. The things that hold us in a trance whenever that guy comes around. That's what holds our attention. So, we choose based on those things."

Kenya paused to think. She wanted to be sure that she got her point across because she knew that to Merrick, Patrice was one of the three women who mattered. Her, his moms and his baby sister. So, she needed her to understand her reality.

"Merrick isn't like these other guys out here, he's not a dope boy. The dope game doesn't define Merrick. He is not a thug or gangster. So, it's not a gang or certain group of people that defines him. Merrick is just Merrick. He'd be defined by the way he thinks more than by how he looks, what he wears, or what kind of truck he drives. I think that I would have noticed him if he wore dirty clothes and drove a pinto because he'd do something that would just say, *Hey, my names Merrick.*" She glanced sideways at Pat. "Does any of this make any sense to you?"

"Girl, please, I've known Snipes for a few years now. So, I know how easy it is to get caught up," Patrice told her. "But the nigga still fine though." She laughed and Kenya laughed with her.

"So, you're doing all of this to show Snipes that you're not like these other bitches?" Pat asked.

"To show him that there's more to me than a big ass and dimples."

"Yeah, but I bet Snipes hasn't overlooked the ass part," Pat said.

Kenya laughed. "Yeah, but I still get this feeling. It's as if he's waiting for me to prove myself, to shows him that I'm different. So, I'm willing to do this, just to show him that if he and I are going to be down, then we're going to be all the way down. That we can do dirt together. I want to show him that when Biggie sung about him and his bitch, his definition was an outline of me."

They reached the Days Inn and the conversation came to an end. Patrice could say that she honestly looked at this woman a whole lot differently. She was nothing like Snipes' ex, Tasha, that was for sure. She wondered if Merrick knew it.

****

Bradly paced the floor in his office. He wasn't upset or mad about the situation, he was just trying to keep his mind focused on the matter at hand. He recalled someone telling him when he was younger that positive thoughts led to positive results. He was thinking that things in a couple of days, either he would make more money than he'd been making, or something would go wrong. It was one or the other, no middle ground to this equation.

Either way, he still believed in Merrick. He knew that the boy was a competent nigger who was good at following instructions and getting a job done. Their past dealings had proven that. So, if anything went wrong it would be on Vinnie's people. Neither Merrick or Bradly knew these people. He didn't know any of these guys, but Vinnie had assured him that they were both made men.

Bradly didn't really know many made men.

If not for my dumb ass sister marrying into the mob, I wouldn't know a single mad man.

He shook his head in disgust, because in his opinion most of them were big dumb Italians that were more muscle then brains. Very few of them could think. But he didn't worry himself about that at the moment. Vinnie thinks he can just boss me around and not have to answer for it. But I got a plan for that!

Bradly laughed hard. He knew that he was a chess master, while they were mere checkers players. So, now, as he paced in his office, he had high hopes for Merrick and their future dealings. Especially with Merrick being a good nigger and all.

****

"So, what do you think?" Alpha leader asked.

"About what?" Bravo's team leader responded.

Both were sitting inside of a low-budget, Super 8 motel, going over the last-minute details. Their teams were in the other room. Both Alpha team and Bravo team consisted of three men and their leader.

"He says if we can spare the Negro, then to do so," Alpha leader said.

Bravo leader was in the process of loading his semi assault rifle, which was military issued and held a 30-round clip.

"I'm not racist," Bravo leader said. "But I'm not stupid either. Dead people don't make good witnesses."

Bravo leader finished loading the clip and pushed it into the rifle. He then checked the flash grenades. He never went into a mission without his weapons at 100% and even though these people were supposed to not have weapons. He wasn't taking any chances.

****

Merrick went down to the ice machine with the bucket because Kenya had picked up a bottle of Armadale Vodka that she wanted to try. She couldn't drink it straight, so she had to drink it with orange juice and to drink it with orange juice, she had to have ice.

With her prancing around the room in those sheer boy shorts she slept in, he would have walked to Arabia to get her some ice. But he wasn't about to tell her that. He was bending over scooping the ice out when Pat found him.

"I see girlfriend is about to try that Armadale out, huh?"

He turned to find her with an ice pail too. "You must've got you a bottle, too," he said.

"And you know this, man," she laughed, but then there was a moment of silence. "Snipes, can I ask you something?"

"Sure. What's up?" He put on his serious face.

"How do you really look at Kenya?"

He thought about the question a moment. "Truthfully, I think shorty has a whole lot of potential in her that's being suppressed. I think she's really looking for a man that she can trust and give her all to. But, hey, I could be wrong. Maybe she's just like every other girl but she's just better at hiding it."

Patrice was quiet for a minute. "Nah, she's definitely not like every other female."

"Oh, yeah? You must know something I don't."

"If I tell you, then you'll have to promise not to let on that I told you."

"Girl this is me you're talking to. Don't I know the secrets you keep from your own man?"

"Uh, good point," she agreed then she told him all about their girl bonding moment. And everything that Kenya told her.

****

"Whooo." Kenya shook like she had the chills and Merrick watched as the goose bumps popped up on her arms. She'd just taken a good sip of her drink, which he had mixed for her himself.

"I think ya put too much vodka in it," she said.

Merrick laughed. "Nah, yo soft ass just ain't built like that." He watched as her head rolled sideways on her neck and shoulders. Looking too sexy for TV.

"Nigga, ain't nothing soft about me but my ass. Just wait, I'ma show yo tough ass," she stated.

He couldn't help but laugh again. "Listen, love, do you know why I haven't tried to sex you, yet?" He watched as she shook her head. They were reclined on the bed, sipping their drinks. "It's not because I don't want to. Trust me, I definitely want to, but I also need you to be mine completely. I know that nigga shattered yo trust and with most women, when that happens, they don't give 100% of themselves to the next nigga.

"I know that I'm a good nigga, but I can't just tell you that and as a good nigga, I won't accept anything less than 100% from a good woman. Something tells me you're a good, strong black woman. The kind of woman I'd want to give life to my seeds, but I don't want you and another nigga'z drama, I want you. If we have some drama, then let it be drama between us," he stated and he could see that she felt his pain.

CHAPTER TEN

Love is love and I enjoy the love, but when there's conflict, then it destroys the love, you can't toy with love niggaz take it to the heart, you ain't gone find too many niggaz willing to back in the dark... Keep it real from the start. Don't fuck it up now, later on don't even hit me like fuck it up how... You my dog and I'd die for you let's keep it like that, give me unconditional love and I'm giving it right back.—DMX Where's my Dogg

It was 6 p.m. when Patrice pulled the used Toyota on to the street and a little down from the loading dock. For a minute, they all sat inside the car in silence. There was no need to speak, the plan had already been laid out.

Ameed, wearing the extra vest, had both .44's on him. Since Merrick couldn't take his gun in, Ameed decided to take it. He also had an Ithica Mag 10 shotgun that Merrick had bought off somebody. The shotgun was so powerful that it only loaded three shotgun shells but those shells were scatter shots. One shot would take down two or three people standing only a few feet apart and it was loud, it sounded like thunder. Merrick had also found a lady's' edition 380, but it only had two clips, he gave those to Kenya. Those, along with her 9mm and its four clips would be enough for any problem.

****

Stuart held his arm up and looked at the time on his watch. The customs people were late and until they came, their move couldn't be made. He looked to where the black guy, who they called Walt, was sitting at a table, smoking a cigarette. Ned was walking around, doing perimeter checks of the warehouse.

Walt looked up at him. "They're late. Should be here soon, though." He hunched his shoulders like he didn't care.

Stuart was really starting to like this guy, but just as the thought came to him, the light blue sedan with US Customs on its side, pulled up. They watched as a woman and a man stepped out. The woman held a clip board in her hand but they both had police issued 9mm's on their hips, along with their badges.

Stuart asked his people to stay out of their way so that they could do their jobs more effectively.

****

After the customs people pulled in Ameed said, "That was them that just pulled up."

"But their late," Kenya pointed out.

Just before Ameed could comment on the customs people being late, they watched as two H-2 hummers pulled up to the loading docks. Both trucks stopped and what looked like two military teams jumped out. They continued to watch as the team launched two flash grenades into the warehouse then started filling into it by twos.

"Ameed, somethings wrong," Kenya said.

"I know." He watched as the men went inside.

"Well, we better do something. Merrick is in there by himself," she replied.

Ameed was trying to get his thoughts together. He wasn't sure if the customs people had called in back up or not, he didn't know what to do yet.

"Fuck it!" Kenya gripped the door handle and opened her door. "I'm not about to let my man go out bad!" But before

Ameed could say anything she was out of the car running across the street.

"Ameed! Go with her!" Pat yelled.

It seemed like her words forced the extra juices in him to start flowing. Ameed pushed his door open and came out with the Ithica.

****

The flash grenade hit with a loud bang and there was an extremely bright light. As soon as the bang went off, Merrick's instincts kicked in. That and his fear of going to prison. In one smooth motion, he fell back in his chair, his cigarette hit the floor and he rolled to the side. When the bright light illuminated the warehouse, he closed his eyes and the headache came instantly as he listened.

"Move! Move! Secure the perimeter!"

Shots rang out. His headache got worst.

"Somebody's got a gun! Cover, cover!"

A few more shots rang out. They must have overlooked the customs agent's guns but whoever it was that was raiding the warehouse, Merrick realized that they were serious and weren't playing any games. He wasn't about to put himself in the open like that.

Why hadn't he brought the bottle of Tylenol threes?

****

Kaboom!

Ameed came through the door and bust open at the first group of men he saw. He asked no questions, spun the shot gun to the other side and squeezed again.

Kaboom!

Ameed stepped into the warehouse after he cut down several of the military style team. Kenya was right behind him, holding down the back. He looked over his shoulder at her. "Take one of the .44's and find Snipes!" he instructed.

She didn't hesitate, Kenya pulled the .44 out of his waist at the back, along with two of the clips. Then she moved deeper into the warehouse.

In Ameed's eyes, anybody that wasn't black was an enemy. He would deal with them as such. Once he'd let off the last shell from the shot gun, he dropped it and pulled out the .44, continuing to leave bodies behind him. *If only Snipes was on the scene*, he thought.

Kenya found Merrick behind the overturned table. "Are you alright?"

"Yeah." Merrick caught his breath. "But what's going on, who are these people?"

"We don't know. We just saw them raid the warehouse and I wasn't about to leave you in here by yourself," Kenya explained. "Are you hurt? Can you move?"

He wasn't going to tell her the truth. Around them the gun fight continued and they couldn't tell who was winning. "Yeah, I'm good."

"A'ight," Kenya said. Then she pulled out the .44 and handed it to him with the extra clips. "Because Ameed is out there by himself. We need to take care of this problem," she paused to look at his eyes, she noticed that they looked grey. "Are you with me or not?"

Merrick looked deep into her eyes and it was at that moment that he wondered if something was wrong. He made his mind up at that moment, Kenya was his woman and there wasn't any other way to look at it. "Yeah. Let's see what this business is about."

He clutched the gun, took a few breaths and then pushed up from the floor. He came up letting off shots but he wasn't shooting blindly. Merrick tried his best to make every shot count for something and Kenya was right beside him. Together they moved throughout the warehouse taking down anything in their way. If it looked hostile, it received a bullet.

The shootout lasted five and a half minutes after Merrick joined in. When all the shots stopped, he called out, "Yo, Meed!"

"Peace, God! You good?" Ameed asked.

"Yeah, we good," Merrick said.

Ameed stepped out of the shadows and looked around really good before he walked over to where Merrick and Kenya stood. It looked like he started to say something but didn't. "Man, what the fuck was that all about?"

Merrick took a good look around. He saw that both Stuart and Ned were dead, along with the two US customs agents and an uncounted number of Military dressed men. "I don't know, but we can't hang out here." He paused when his eyes landed on the 42 bags of money that were still sitting in the middle of the floor. "Kenya, go tell Pat ta back the car up to the docking port and pop the trunk."

Kenya didn't even stop to ask questions; she turned and ran at high speed.

Merrick then turned and looked at Ameed. "Yo, we taking everything!"

Ameed looked at the 42 bags, trying to figure out how it would all fit into the Toyota. But the car was already being backed up and Kenya jumped out.

"Hurry up, we ain't got all night!" she shouted.

Ameed looked over at Merrick. "Everything?"

Merrick was already tucking his gun. "I said everything, didn't I?"

Together they loaded all of the bags into the Toyota and five minutes later they were leaving the scene of the crime. Them and the 42 bags.

When they reached the Days Inn, there wasn't time to check out. Instead, they transferred all 42 bags to the Escalade and the Lexus. While that was being done, Kenya and Pat were in the rooms packing their things. The whole process took no more than 15 minutes and they were on their way to highway 95 north.

"So, what do you think happen?" Ameed asked.

Kenya was driving, while Merrick sat in the passenger seat and smoked two cigarettes back to back. His phone was on the dashboard but it was on speaker.

"Fuck if I know," Merrick stated.

"How many people knew about the job?" Ameed's voice came from the phone.

"As far as I know," Merrick said. "Just Bradly and the people he got the info from."

"Then one of them set you up," Ameed stated.

Merrick thought about it, his head was pounding. "Why do you think it was a set up? Maybe the customs people called in backup," he speculated.

"Bruh, you're smarter than that," Ameed said. "Did anyone yell police?"

"Nah." His hand shook as he pulled out the pill bottle.

"When we came in, it didn't look like nobody was trying to arrest anybody. Whoever those people were, they weren't legal. They came to kill and on top of that, they knew what they were doing. Think about it, the flash grenade?" Ameed said.

Merrick remembered, the hit team had come in pretty hard and were surprised to realize that the customs agents had guns. So, whoever they worked for had told them the security guards wouldn't have guns. That meant it was someone on the inside.

"So, what do you wanna do, Snipes?" Ameed asked.

Merrick looked over at Kenya. He opened the bottle as she glanced at him, having felt his eyes on her.

"I'm with you, whatever you do," she said.

He nodded, poured eight pills into his hand and popped them all at once.

"Me and Pat are down too. All you gotta do is say the word Snipes," Ameed agreed.

The entire time he'd been wondering if Bradly had sold him out. Then when the news hit that his body hadn't turned up and all of the money was missing, there would be a problem. But, if it wasn't Bradly and his connection put the cross down, he didn't know how that would play out. He chewed the pills and swallowed.

"The first thing we gone do is get a couple rooms when we get back. We need to see how much money we've got before we finalize the plan. But for now, you and Pat relax and enjoy the ride. I need to talk to Kenya," Merrick told them.

****

Miami police pulled up on the scene not long after Merrick and his team left. It took them at least two hours to put the pieces together.

"So, someone got away with a lot of money," one of the cops said.

Another one was looking over the Brinks invoice. "According to this," the one with the invoice was saying, "more like 88 million in old bills. All $50's and hundred-dollar bills."

"Might as well put an APB out."

"On what? We don't even have a description of the sup-posed suspects," the one officer said.

"Just put it out anyway!"

So, the officer walked off to put out the APB. What he really wanted to ask was why they had undercover Georgia GBI agents dead in the warehouse. That's what had him shook up. They knew the deal with Brinks and the overseas banks. This wasn't the first time the Federal Reserve had taken a hit, but it was the first time that they'd lost every last bit of the money at once, with no leads.

There hadn't been a heist this big since the John F Kennedy International Airport heist in 1978, when the perp's got away with $8 million. Now this, it had to be Mafia related. So, when he put the APB out, he made sure to stress that they were looking for either white males or Italians. Because that was the only thing that made sense.

****

They made it through the toll booths with no problem and when they were less than 25 miles from Augusta when Merrick called again.

"Yo," Ameed said.

"Listen," Merrick began. "Until I can figure out what's going on, we can't go home. So, we're going to get on I-20 and head to Atlanta. When we hit the city, I'll tell y'all what we gone do."

"A'ight, we with you, bruh," Ameed said.

They hit I-20 and proceeded straight to Atlanta Ga.

I-285 was the local perimeter that encircled a major por-tion of the Metro Atlanta area. At first, when they got onto it, they weren't sure where to go. The sun was up and it was

Thursday. Merrick exited 285 onto Glenwood Road, right where the flea market was located. He by passed the Super 8 and pulled into the Old English Hotel.

Once inside the parking lot, both Kenya and Pat went inside to get two rooms and as it turned out they ended up with two honeymoon suites. It took them several trips back and forth to get all 42 bags into Merrick's room and although they paid for two rooms, they eventually put the do not disturb sign out and all fell asleep in the same bed. They decided that they would deal with reality when they woke up.

****

Bradly didn't know what to think. The Miami Police weren't releasing a whole lot of information and all he knew was that they had identified some GBI agents from Augusta in the warehouse, dead. They wouldn't tell him anything else so he was in the dark on the details.

Trai'Quan

88

CHAPTER ELEVEN

Comin through like I do, you know getting my bark on, kinda knew she a thug cause when I met her she had a scarf on...—DMX How It's Going Down

She didn't exactly know what woke her up, but when she opened her eyes Kenya found herself looking up into Merrick's eyes. He'd been watching her sleep.

"Is something wrong?"

"Nah, ma. I was just appreciating your beauty, that's all."

Kenya smiled. "Oh, yeah, and what about my beauty holds your attention the most?"

He acted like he was really thinking about it. "It's got to be yo ass. That muthafucka would stop all traffic if you had on the right shit."

"Mmhm..."

"But, yo, we gone make it, ma," he stated.

"I'll be glad when y'all get your own room," Ameed said from the other side of the bed. "Cause y'all killing me with all this corny shit."

"I've got to agree," said Pat. "So, what's up with breakfast?"

"We can't go out and leave these bags so we're gone have to order from room service. After that, this is the deal. Me and Ameed gone have to go get rid of the truck and car. Bradly should have my tag number for the truck so we gone have to get some new rides. Then while we're out, you ladies gone be counting this money. We'll also buy some suitcases to put it in. Those bags are too noticeable. Everybody good with that?" He asked.

No one had any problems with his plan.

The first thing they did was burn the Lexus. Then they went to a GMC Dealership where they were given a good deal on the trade for the Escalade. In return, they purchased two Yukon Denali's, both were 2009 models. One was midnight blue while the other was a deep, dark green. Merrick quickly put dibs on the green one.

After spending part of the day at the dealership, they went to the closest department store and purchased several large suitcases. When they were finally finished, Merrick insisted that they ride around Atlanta for a while. He wanted to get the feel of it and was also looking for something. He was thinking that they would probably all need to move out of Augusta. He didn't know for sure how much money they had, but he did know it was too much to keep hidden in Augusta. Somebody would notice it, plus he needed to get his moms and Jen out of that place, at least until he found out who pulled the dummy move on the job.

He stopped in Glenwood Mills, in South Fulton and wrote down the number from one of the For-Sale signs in the yard of a house. He had actually seen some houses that were all on the same street, but he would need to call the people and see what the actual ticket on them would be. He would also have to send Ameed and Patrice back to Augusta, to get his moms and Jen. Merrick knew that he needed to do all of this within the week since Bradly was a cop. It wouldn't be long before he found out that Merrick was missing, so his moms and sister needed to disappear, ASAP.

****

Vincent was able to get a little more information than Bradly, when he called. Mostly because the mafia actually had people in just about every major city. Miami was major because the entire state of Florida was a tourist state, but Vincent was not happy with what his people told him.

The fact that the GBI agents found dead at the scene were from Augusta was enough to piss him off. As soon as he heard the news, he knew Bradly had tried to double cross him. Yet, something had gone wrong. All of the agents were dead and there weren't any black kids present. Vincent would hate to believe that one black kid was that damn good. Good enough to kill all of those people, steal nearly 100 million in cash and then vanish without a trace. That fast?

Vincent thought that if he was that good, then maybe he should have that nigger on his team. One way or the other, somebody pulled a double cross and right now, it was looking like Bradly was eating too much green food.

Vincent hated green foods. They reminded him too much of envy. Envy was green and money was green. In fact, his missing money had been green and he needed to find it.

****

"It's about seventy-five million," Patrice said.

"Uh-un, girl, I counted eighty," Kenya stated.

Both Merrick and Ameed stood by the window, talking while smoking a blunt. Already they'd taken the 42 bags to a dumpster far away. They used box cutters to shred them and removed all names before putting them in the dumpsters.

"Alright. So, you want me and Pat to go get Ms. Tiffany and Jennifer. Then what?" Ameed asked.

"You bring them back here. Don't let them bring any clothes or anything big. Just tell them to get whatever ID they need and come up here," Merrick explained to him. "While you're gone, I'll be working on something else, it shouldn't take you but a few hours."

From Atlanta to Augusta on I-20 was only a two-hour drive, so going and coming back would be four hours.

"What about my moms and Pats?" Ameed asked.

"Well, since Bradly doesn't know anything about either of you, they shouldn't be in any danger. However, you will be taking enough money to give your moms and hers, so they'll be comfortable," Merrick explained.

"A'ight. That's good. So, when do you want us to leave?"

"First thing in the morning," Merrick said. "Bradly knows I live with my moms and sister. He'll be on to them within the next 72 hours, they need to vanish quickly."

There was simply no other way to do it, not when he couldn't tell where the real threat was coming from. He still had to figure out how he was going to deal with it.

****

"Tell me something, Brad, I need to be able to understand what's going on here and right now I'm thinking you're the only one that can explain it to me." Vincent's voice came through the phone's ear piece.

Bradly leaned back in his custom recliner; he had been sitting in his den when the call came. Sitting in there thinking, trying to put the pieces together. There was something that wasn't adding up completely. He sat back in the chair and looked up at the ceiling fan as it slowly turned above his head.

"Vincent, I'm afraid this is one of those times when you're not going to hear what you want to hear," Bradly told him.

"And what is it that you think I want to hear?" Vincent asked in a hard voice.

"I'd imagine that you want me to tell you that everything will be alright, that the money will turn up and we'll split it. Yada, yada, yada. But I can't tell you that, because I have no idea where the money could be."

"And your guy?" Vincent asked.

It was Saturday, Bradly now knew that Merrick's body wasn't found inside the warehouse. In fact, everybody that was found in the warehouse, happen to be white. Not one of them were black.

"Unless your people got rid of him, I have no idea if he's even alive," Bradly told him. What he didn't tell Vincent was that he'd sent some people to his mother's house out in Georgetown. It seemed that both the mother and daughter, were now missing, which could only mean one thing. From what his officers told him, they had left in a rush, leaving behind everything, clothes, jewelry, etc.

"Do you have any possible leads on him?" Vincent asked.

"Not a one." he sighed.

"What about family and friends?"

"Family has disappeared and this guy didn't hang with anyone else that I know of. I'm still looking into it," Bradly explained.

"Well, here's what I'm going to do," Vincent began. "I have this guy, he will be leaving for Georgia in a few minutes. This guy will contact you once he gets there, he may be able to help you in your search. And, Bradly, you had better hope that he can."

Bradly's face twisted up. He wanted to ask Vincent who the fuck he thought he was, threatening a cop? That didn't even sound right, but as the phone went dead, he didn't feed into it. However, he was wondering how Merrick had been able to pull it off. He'd never acted that smart before and he'd never seen any unusual intellectual qualities in the nigger. So, Bradly simply could not figure out how Merrick was able to out think him. It just didn't make sense.

****

His name was Evan George, he had two first names and couldn't logically figure out why his mother had named him like that. Usually a child was named after another relative and even then, it would be by last name, even that wasn't the case with him. Yet, Evan George was of good Sicilian breeding. He was from the old country; however, they didn't call Evan by his Christian name here in the States. Here, they referred to him as Bumpy and throughout Brooklyn that's what people called him, Bumpy.

He got the nickname because of his size and the size of his hands. Body wise, one would think that he should have been a wrestler. Standing at 6'8" and 380lbs, he wasn't fat or out of shape. His hands were unusually large, in fact they were so big that he couldn't do some things with them. However, his hands were perfect for other things and Bumpy liked doing other things with his hands.

He especially liked to do things to women with his hands. But he wasn't being sent to Georgia to deal with a woman, he was being sent there to deal with what Vinnie had called a *miscommunication of sorts*. When Vinnie deemed something to be a miss-anything, it usually meant problems for the one who missed something.

****

Miami Police Department really didn't know how to respond when FBI agent Chester Simkins took over the case.

Simkins was a 20-year veteran who looked like anything but an FBI agent. At 5'11", he was brown skinned with salt and pepper hair and wore Dapper Dan suits that didn't scream cop. He looked more like a 48-year-old street hustler that grew up listening to hip hop and watching mob movies.

"So, who's going to run it down to me?" Agent Simkins asked as he stepped onto the scene.

The lead investigator looked at agent Simkins with a little more emotion than he needed to because he already knew the situation. Due to it being such a large heist, Brinks enlisted the Federal Bureau of Investigations.

"Shouldn't you have a partner? I mean for such a big case like this," the officer asked

Agent Simkins smiled. He wore a full goatee and it was trimmed with a thin lining. He also had one open faced, gold tooth and wore an expensive watch. It looked like a Philp Stein time piece.

"Yeah, I've got a partner, but right now my partner is having a word with the Director of your South Florida High Intensity Drug Trafficking department. That's neither here nor there. So, who's gonna talk to me?" he asked, as he looked around.

The officer waved for another investigator to come over and they both explained everything they knew to Agent Simkins. Afterward, they walked him through the crime scene, step by step, pointing out various things.

"What about the shotgun?" Agent Simkins asked. "It's an Ithica Mag 10, right? That kind of gun is hard to come by on the streets. What came up on it?"

"Well, the gun was clean. There were no prints and its serial numbers were removed," an officer said. "More than likely, it was bought off the streets, probably from some drug dealer. So, it's a dead end."

Agent Simkins didn't think so, but he kept his comments to himself. "And this extra temp worker, what was his name?"

"Guy named Walt Freeman. But the Temp said they didn't send an extra guy over and we received no hits on a guy by that name," the officer informed him. "There is one thing, though."

"Oh, yeah?" Agent Simkins looked up.

"We found some cigarette butts and our people were able to get a partial print off one of them. So far, the partial doesn't match anyone at the scene. We're running it through our data base now, but we haven't received a hit yet."

"Have your people send it over to the Federal Building. We've got a larger search engine and this guy may not be from this state," Agent Simkins said.

He looked over the scene again, twelve bodies in all. Eight of them were GBI, two belonged to US customs and two were Brinks security personnel. There was also a set of finger prints that didn't fit.

He thought this one might be a hard case to crack. Then again, he was the best at what he did.

CHAPTER TWELVE

He didn't buy the three hours he intended to, but when Ameed returned with his mother and sister, Merrick felt better knowing they were safe. He would be able to think a little clearer. His moms had just pointed out, after seeing all of the money in the room, that if he started spending large amounts of money, he would be spending some quality time with his father. She said the FBI would lock in on it, especially if they were looking for it. She had assumed that they had robbed a bank or something, but she didn't ask too many questions.

Tiffany Blackmon was from the heart of Camden, NJ. She knew the codes of the streets and she lived by them without having to be told.

Merrick ended up having his moms, Kenya and Patrice lease three condos over by North Leg Mall. They were called The Heist and the one-bedroom units went for $1200, which Kenya and Pat leased while his moms leased a two-bedroom condo in his sister's name. He had explained that he expected someone to try to find him through her name, so she used his sister's name. Each one of them also purchased their own SUV's by making down payments, no one was supposed to buy straight out. That would draw too much attention.

Kenya got a white, 2008, Lexus RX 300. Patrice got the 2008 Infiniti Qx4 in red and his moms used Jen's name to get a black, 2008, Sequoia. They had all leased to own.

Merrick had also given each one of them enough money to furnish the condos, but even the furniture was leased to own. The only thing that they were allowed to straight out pay for was their clothes and for two weeks straight, he sent them to North Leg Mall and South DeKalb Mall.

He had his moms enroll Jen in North DeKalb High school, which she seemed to be alright with. He also had both Kenya and Patrice enroll at Agnes Scott Women's college, he wanted them to take classes in finances. The way he explained it, there was just too much money involved to not have a full proof plan. A full proof plan consisted of *knowing* how to invest, move and bank money successfully.

Amazingly, setting all of that into motion hadn't taken more than a million dollars and the numbers weren't 70 or 75 million, they were 88 million on the head. So, while all of this was going on, Merrick and Ameed were going into the second stage of his plan.

****

"Girl, you gone get the door or not?" Zoe asked.

"Nigga, you act like you're doing something important," Li'l Mama stated.

All he was doing at the moment was sitting at the kitchen table, cutting up the ounce he'd just paid for, but she walked over to the door and opened it anyway.

When she did, Li'l Mama smiled, both Merrick and Ameed were standing there in front of her, looking brand new.

"Damn, baby girl, I wish I could catch you without that nigga, Zoe, being around. I might try to get you to cheat," Merrick joked.

"What?" Zoe called out. "That had better be that nigga, Snipes or Ameed, any other nigga gone get it."

Merrick hugged her and stepped into the apartment as Ameed did the same. They walked into the kitchen where Zoe sat with his dope.

Quiet Money

"Nigga." Merrick moved to scoop up all of the dope and brush it back into the bag then he held it up in front of him. Everyone was looking at him holding the bag. "Listen, Zoe, being up in here, pushing this shit ain't cool. Don't you know you putting ole girl and her kids at risk?"

"Yeah. But shit, Snipes, a nigga gotta eat," Zoe said as he looked at his bag. "Man, you know I've got too many strikes against me. I been to prison twice, I've got a punk ass GED and nothing but hustling skills. What am I going to do?"

Merrick looked over at Li'l Mama but all she could do was drop her head. "How much you making off this, Zoe?"

"About $1800."

"A'ight, Ameed give Li'l Mama two grand for me," Merrick instructed, then he took the dope into the bathroom and flushed it. When he came back out, Li'l Mama was counting the money and Zoe was looking stupid. "Listen," Merrick started. "I've got a job for you, but it ain't selling dope or crack. But to do the job, I'll need you both to pack up your shit and move to Atlanta."

Zoe looked from him to Ameed. "Is he serious?"

Ameed nodded his head.

"What kind of job and when we gotta be in the A?" Zoe asked.

"It's an easy job and you won't be putting Li'l Mama and the babies at risk. You make what, four grand a week, selling crack?" Merrick asked.

"Shit, if that, sometimes," Zoe admitted.

"A'ight. You move to Atlanta and work for me. I'll start you off at five grand a month and I'll give Li'l Mama $2,500."

"Hell yeah!" Li'l Mama spoke up. "When do you want us to move?"

"Today," Merrick said.

"What, nigga? What about my furniture and everything else," she asked.

Merrick glanced around the apartment and then back at her. He reached into his jacket and pulled out an envelope that was 10x13 inches and handed it to her. "That should cover anything you leave. What it doesn't, I'll replace when you get to the A. But I need y'all to leave some time tonight. Me and Ameed are leaving around 6:00, we'll swing back through for you." He looked at both of them. "Put the kids in your van and be ready to pull out. Trust me, everything's going to be alright."

Li'l Mama nearly fainted when she looked in the envelope. Zoe glanced over her shoulder, he didn't know what these niggaz were up to, but he wanted in.

****

"Merrick, boy, where have you been?" Tammy screamed and hugged him.

"Here and there. Taking care of some business, but how have you been?"

Her spirit dropped. "I lost my job when I couldn't keep a ride. When you left, I didn't know what happened," she said.

"Yeah. Well here, sign this." He handed her a piece of paper and she looked at it.

"What, your selling me a car? Nigga, I can't buy no car," she told him.

"Just sign the damn paper, girl."

He watched as she signed it then he turned and waved his hand. Ameed open the door of the 2001 Benz, E320 and walked over. He handed the keys to her.

"Listen," Merrick said. "We're leaving for Atlanta around 6:00, I've got a job for you if you want it. It's legal and you'll be making something like five grand a month. Oh, yeah, here." He paused to pull out a 10x13 envelope and handed it to her before he continued. "Pack up whatever you can get in the Benz. If it won't fit, leave it. Move to Atlanta with me and we gone get money. But it's on you. If you're not ready when we come by, then so be it. Keep everything, it's my gift," he explained.

Tammy had already decided that she and her son were leaving when he came through.

****

Both JT and Hightower were sitting on the hood of the 89 Fleetwood Cadillac they had put their money together to buy. They were listening to music while they watched the trap. Neither one solid crack, all they sold was weed.

When the Denali pulled up, they were trying to figure out who had a ride like that until they saw Merrick and Ameed get out.

"Damn, you niggaz done fuckin' came up," JT said.

"Yeah. Big money," Hightower added.

Merrick laughed. He had always liked these niggaz. "Listen, I've got a job if you niggaz think you real enough to handle it," he said then waited as they looked at one another.

Together, they both broke out in laughter as if Merrick didn't really hear his own joke.

"Shit, what we gotta do?" Hightower asked.

Merrick handed them a 10x13 inch envelope. "Pack your shit, anything that can't fit in your ride, leave it. Be ready to move to Atlanta and we'll be back through here about 6:30. If you ain't ready, you lose out."

He went back to the Denali where he and Ameed left. They had one more stop and then they would be on their way back to his team. Merrick wasn't sure if they would be able to make it work, but they were damn sure about to try. Especially if they could get this last person on the team. He had a plan, one where everyone could eat and he might be able to dodge that bullet that was aimed at him. This would be part two to his movie.

CHAPTER THIRTEEN

Remember rapping duke, da ha da ha, you never thought that hip hop would take it this far... Now I'm in the lime light because I rhyme tight, time to blow up like the world trade bomb center, the opposite of a beginner...— Biggie—Juicy 1994

Credit Suisse was one of Switzerland's most prestigious and powerful banks. Their clientele was so exclusive that they didn't accept too small of a deposit. They were a grand bank that also catered to smaller banks. It was such an old bank that certain things were done more out of the respect of their long-standing existence and extreme confidence.

The two well-dressed men, wearing their expensive business suits entered the bank. Both of them were holding handles that were connected to the tow along bags that they pulled behind them. Due to the fact that these gentlemen looked the part of businessmen, nothing seem out of the ordinary with them. No one stopped to speculate about them and the two large suit cases that they pulled.

They arrived at a desk where a fairly young secretary sat, typing something on her computer's keypad. The woman looked up as they stopped at her desk.

"Hi, welcome to Credit Suisse. My name is Susan. How may I be of assistance to you gentlemen?"

She watched as the taller of the two men stepped forward. "We would like to make a rather sizable deposit," he stated.

"Oh, well deposits are made at window number three."

"Yeah, well about that. I believe we'll have to see the manager to complete this business transaction. It is rather large."

The manager stood behind his desk with his left arm folded across his chest. His right elbow in its crook and the palm of his right hand holding his chin. The emotion he was experiencing at the moment wasn't confusion. He wasn't confused, it was more like shock and surprise. He looked from the two men in his office, back down to the two open suit cases.

"Well?" The one who called himself Merrick asked.

"Uh. Yes, I'll have to have my people count it, but you say there's 60 million here?" The manager asked again. "And you do understand how we do business here. The relationship between us here, at Credit Suisse, and the customer is strictly personal," he explained.

"Exactly and that's why we chose Credit Suisse," Merrick said.

"Yes, well, there's also the matter of who will have access to this account," the manager said.

"The two of us. We want the account set up in the names of Merrick and Ameed Blackson."

The manager nodded. "And you both have identification to this effect?" He watched as they pulled out their wallets and let him check their license and passports. Once he was satisfied, he handed them back, then buzzed his secretary in.

"Yes, Mr. Alric?" She asked.

"Mary, could you get someone and have this money counted. We've just acquired two new clients."

They watched as her eyes became big, looking at the money. Then she looked back at them, almost as if to ask, who are these guys?

****

APRIL 2009

M&A Limousine services was located on Moorland Rd. It was once a Mexican bar that sat between the Federal prison and a truck stop, but all of that area had been remodeled now, with an extension to the parking lot. Out in the side and back area of the lot there was an Escalade stretch limo, an H-2 stretch limo, a Lincoln Navigator stretch limo and a Range Rover stretch limo. All were a part of the exclusive SUV line. Other than that, there were two Mercedes Benz stretch limos and two Lexus stretch limos, all of which were custom designed. All came with several TV's DVD players, PlayStation 2's and fully stocked bars.

The company had grown quickly over its short time in existence, into being known for catering to the ballers, rappers and even the dope boys. Everything about M&A limousine service was legal.

Ameed pulled the navigator limo into the parking lot and around to the back where each limo had its own parking space. He parked the Navigator then got out. As he was making his way across the parking lot to the building, he noticed that both JT and Hightower were still out. They were driving the Escalade and Hummer limos, while Snipes drove the range rover and Zoe drove one of the Mercedes limos. They also had Tammy driving one of the Lexus limos and a real light skinned girl that was part Latino, named Gina. Snipes had pulled her out of Foxy Lady's, a strip club not far up the street.

Snipes had run into her at the truck stop one day while buying gas and he noticed that she had a very exotic look for a Latina. He had started a conversation and eventually she assumed he was trying to hit on her. She got offended but when they parted ways, Snipes followed her to the club.

A few days, he had checked her out and found out she wasn't on drugs, that she had two kids and a dead-beat baby's daddy. Snipes and he pulled up at the club and Snipes offered her a job. He even moved her into the Heist.

The Heist seemed to have become their stomping grounds. All of them had condos in it. Tammy and her son, JT and Hightower had one each. But he'd had to get Zoe and Lil Mama into a nice four-bedroom house not far from the condos. Gina also had a three-bedroom house.

Ameed stepped inside of the building and saw Ms. Blacksun and Li'l Mama at the desk talking.

"How you ladies doing?"

"We fine," Ms. Blacksun said.

Her name was Blacksun but in truth, Blackmon was her maiden name. In Augusta, she would have been known under her husband's name, which she could still use and it was Stokes. So, anyone looking for Tiffany Stokes wouldn't find her. Blackmon was changed to Blacksun.

"Oh, Ameed." Li'l Mama stopped him as he was headed to the back to take a shower and change. "You've got an 8:00 p.m. They requested you," she told him.

He pretty much already knew who it was and continued to the back. The building consisted of a large lounge area where the drivers could relax and chill when they weren't working. There was also a universal gym, which he, Snipes, JT, Hightower and Zoe used every chance they got. The girls also used it, but not as much as the guys did.

Ameed stripped down in the locker area and put his used suit on the hanger for Li'l Mama to get. The way it was set up, they each had a number of suits, all of them either Roberta Cavali, Brooks Brothers, Alexandre Birman, Sergio Ross, Fendi or Prada.

Snipes said they were professionals, so they had to look and act professional. He had three basic rules when working. Rule #1: No drinking on the job. Their insurance wouldn't cover it if they had an alcohol level that was at a certain point. So, Snipes said not to risk it. Rule #2: Always be presentable at all times. Which meant the expensive suits. And rule #3: Never speak unless spoken to. Snipes said it was a job, we weren't here to make friends, our goal was to make money.

Ameed stepped into the shower. He had the water turned up high and as hot as he could get it so it could relax his muscles. While under the water, he thought about his 8:00 p.m. It had to be Princess, who was also a stripper at the Foxy Lady.

Princess had what she called her sponsor's, she wouldn't say that she was a call girl. Princess had a few high-profile guys that she dated and they would take her out and spend crazy money on her. The funny part about it was that she rarely slept with them. Most of them were older men who had a lot of money and none of them were from Atlanta. So, whenever they would fly into the city, Princess would call and ask for Ameed.

His relationship with Princess was kind of funny because they did have sex. But, not relationship sex. They were more along the lines of what people called cut buddies. The main reason Princess called on Ameed was because she said that she felt safe with him because she saw him stop a nigga from molesting one of the girls at the club. Well, he thought. At least it never got back to Pat.

On the other side of the courthouse building was a building that leased out office space to the basic law community. Merrick parked his Denali there and exited it. He then walked into the building, kindly nodding his head at several people. He stopped at the elevators, he had already hit the up button and when the elevator arrived, he stepped onto it and then pressed the number eight. He stood there while the elevator rose.

When it reached the eighth floor the doors opened onto an exclusive floor. What made it exclusive was the large gold plat that read Howard & Gibson Attorneys at Law. The entire eighth floor was occupied by twelve law offices and desks for their secretaries. Ten of these lawyers were fresh out of law school, whereas the two senior lawyers were Julius Howard and Marion Gibson. They both had large offices at the far end of each hallway. Julius had five lawyers under him and Marion also had five.

When he arrived at Julius' end of the hallway, the new secretary looked up. A young Muslim sister who belonged to the Nation of Islam.

"Assalam Alaikum, Sister Shabazz," he said.

She looked up with a smile. "Assalam Alaikum, Brother Merrick. I didn't know you were coming by," she expressed.

"Oh, it's not too important. I just had a few things that I needed Brother Julius' advice on. Is he buys?"

"Just a moment."

He waited while she called his office and then she waved him in. He thanked her then walked in. The inside of this office was totally different from the past office Julius had in Augusta. This one had more space. It was larger and he had every possible law book he could think of. They lined two walls, as if this was a library.

Julius looked up from reading the Law Journal he'd just recently received. "Ah, Merrick. How's it going?"

"I'm not complaining much these days. But how about you?" Merrick asked.

Out of the 28 million that he kept, Merrick had given Julius five million to relocate his firm, enlarge it and hire some new help. He hired some good, young black law students and gave them a shot at helping other blacks. In return, Julius and Marion had given Merrick 15% of the firm. Which meant that anyone that worked for Merrick and could possibly need legal assistance for whatever reason, they were automatically covered.

Julius had also been instrumental in helping Merrick and Ameed start up their limo service. Julius, it seemed knew how to make bad money work for a good cause, but Merrick had to come clean and explain the complete story to him which it seemed Julius had heard about in the news. Happy that it wasn't drug money, Julius had accepted it and become a part of the team. He was also Merrick's legal adviser. Julius had only used another five million to start the limo service and get full insurance coverage. That also included full coverage for all of his workers for a health insurance plan.

Out of the 18 million that was left. Julius had helped him open a business account. What he'd done was show Merrick how to incorporate his name and after a short trip to the Cayman Islands where Merrick put 10 million into the bank, he returned and opened a bank account at the Bank of America.

Then, since everything was set up a certain way, the Cayman bank wired two million into Merrick's account. Coming from a secret trust fund that someone had set up for him upon his 5th birthday. But the trust wouldn't give a full payout until his 21st birthday, which would be in July. Then Merrick would receive another six million by wire transfer. Should anyone try to find out who set up the fund, the trail would disappear somewhere over seas.

****

"So, what can I help you with?" Julius asked.

Before he could fix his mouth to voice his issues, the office door was opened and an extremely attractive dark brown skinned woman entered. She was wearing a suit/skirt outfit by Fendi, along with $1000 heels by Giuseppe Zanotti. Merrick could never get over how fine the woman was, no matter how many times he saw her. She was about 5'8" and maybe 132 pounds, with body measurements of 32-25-38. He knew that she was 53 years old but she didn't look to be over 30.

"Hello, Marion," Merrick said.

Marion, as friendly as ever, especially since she too shared his secret, smiled back. "Hi, Merrick. You're looking healthy."

"Yeah, I still hit the gym four times a week. So how are your kids?"

"A headache. It seems like them living in Atlanta and attending Tucker High school has given them the big head. You know they think we're rich now," she laughed.

Marion had two daughters that were both in high school and they hung out with Jen. They were all in the same age group.

"Since you're here, you may be able to help," he said. Then he told them, "I need to find out everything I can about that crooked cop, Bradly. I need to know about all of his possible illegal connections. So, can I use Luke and Laura?"

Luke and Laura were the investigative team. Their names weren't literally Luke and Laura, it was a joke from the soap opera General Hospital. But their names were Perry North and Julia French. Both of them were black and with the nation of Islam, however, prior to joining the Nation of the law firm, Perry had been an FBI field agent in Texas. Julia had been a CIA agent in Washington D.C. at that time.

They'd met through the nation and eventually put together an investigation firm, which happen to be one of the best in the entire state of Georgia. Julius had been able to offer them an exclusive contract when they'd moved to the Atlanta location.

"Well, you'll have to pay for the expenses," Julius said.

"I mean it's a personal issue. Or at least it would be to them, seeing as we three are the only ones here who know why you need to do this."

"I don't think we have anything real big going on at the moment," Marion said.

"Good," Merrick said. "Tell them their covered for expenses, bill it to me or front them the startup fee and you guys bill me. My Queen will get the money to you."

"Consider it done then," Julius said.

Merrick was thinking that he should have put somebody on it. But he'd gone through so much to cover his tracks that he hadn't worried about it. Something told him it would never be over until he found out who else was in the kitchen baking that cake with Bradly.

CHAPTER FOURTEEN

Kenya gasp as Merrick gripped her by the hips and turned her around. The move in itself pressed her belly into the sink and she started to protest, but she didn't, she felt the bathroom sink under her.

She'd initially come into the bathroom to piss on a stick and had seen what she already knew, the evidence that she was indeed pregnant. When Merrick found her there, she didn't even have time to tell him that she was pregnant, she just swept everything she had on the sink onto the floor. She spread her palms on the sink and got ready to receive him. Merrick slid both of his hands down her body. She still had the short skirt on and was still standing in the Minola Blanik Heels. He quickly undid his pants and let them fall to the floor.

There was just something about that big, pretty ass that did something to him. Merrick thrust his right hand down and under her thong. He found her entrance and slid two fingers deep into her wetness. Kenya moaned as she thrust her ass backwards, pushing into his hand, drawing the fingers deeper. He caressed her inner walls and in the process of doing that, his thumb slid across her anus. This was something they tried a few times. Pressing forward, his thumb slipped into her tightness and Kenya moaned louder. She could feel her muscles tighten up and then relax, accepting the alien invasion almost as if she were making a new friend, or meeting an old friend once again.

The double penetration was becoming too intense for her and she was almost to the point of begging. Kenya liked it when he was like this. It was at these times that she knew Merrick was the most passionate with her. She widened her legs just as she began to climax and then she felt the very broad, swollen head of his dick pressing hard into her wetness. Her pussy was already swollen with desire as her sensitive lips parted, allowing him full penetration. She couldn't stop her hips from pushing back to meet him. Both of his hands reached under her and grasp her breast, squeezing them as he plowed deeper into her.

Kenya could feel ever tremor her vaginal muscles made as they contracted. Squeezing and then releasing his dick as if her pussy was breathing and his dick was the air it was trying to breathe more of. While she wasn't moving fast, Merrick was moving deep and strong. Then, as if he couldn't hold it back any longer, he felt himself pumping his seed deep into her and her pussy milked his dick of every last drop that he'd spent.

"Merrick. Baby, I'm pregnant," she whispered.

"And I'm in love," was all that he could say.

They were lying in bed after having made love once more, they were holding one another and talking when he asked, "So how many weeks do you think you are?"

"I'm not sure. I'd guess about six weeks," she replied.

"Well, you need to make an appointment to see a doctor."

Which was something she'd already been thinking about. "So, what do you want? A boy or a girl?"

Merrick thought about it. What did he want? Or did it even matter what the baby was? "You know it don't even matter. I'm just looking forward to being a father."

With that said, they both became quiet. Kenya was thinking about the family they were about to start building.

****

Ameed stepped out of his condo, wearing Phat farm jeans and an En'Ice shirt with a pair of the latest Forces on. He'd left Pat in bed, resting peacefully since she didn't have school today. He walked around her Qx4 and was about to get into his Denali, when a 2009 Porsche, Cayenne Champaign in color, with tinted windows and 22-inch Ashanti rims pulled up behind him. The truck cut off his path and he wouldn't have been able to back out either way. He stood there, about to reach for the .44 that wasn't on him at the moment, when the passenger side window came down. He found himself looking at a white girl who looked like she was in her early 20's with red-blond hair, in curls.

"Your name is Ameed, right?"

"Who's asking?" He returned and watched as the white girl smiled. He knew damn well that he didn't know any white women.

"You've been asking around about a guy. Well, he sent us to bring you to him."

Ameed suddenly remembered what she was talking about. Snipes had told everybody that they weren't to touch any crack, cocaine, heroin, PCP, or Meth. He said he wouldn't back or employ anyone who did but he did leave the door open for two exotic drugs. Marijuana and ecstasy. Especially since a lot of their clientele did it and looked for it. To keep them from having clients that would direct them to drug traps to purchase the drugs, while in the limo's, Snipes had said that Ameed could find them a good source. Thus, he'd heard the name Blaze and asked a few questions.

"Yeah, I have," Ameed said.

"Come on, get in," The white girl said.

Since he really needed this meeting, he went ahead and walked over to the SUV and got into the back seat. It was also at that point when Ameed realized that the girl wasn't white. Behind the wheel driving was a Chinese girl with jet black hair and when he looked at the one on the passenger side closely, he saw that she was Asian, too.

"My name's Kim," the blond said. "And this is Suyi."

"A'ight, I'm Ameed as ya both know."

"Sit back, Ameed. We'll take you to Blaze," Kim said and she did just that.

****

There was a community that was outside of North DeKalb, going into Gwenett. Most of it was on or around Buford Hwy, but it was considered *Little China Town* and the Asians had a very big community there. It consisted of Chinese, Japanese Cambodian and any other types of Asians. Ameed never would have thought it. Being from New York, he'd been to the China town there and it was a little more sophisticated than this one. But yet, this one was still vibrant.

The girl, Suyi, pulled the Cayenne up to a house that was off Buford Hwy and on a street that seemed to be flooded with Chinese gangs. He saw guys hanging around everywhere. They had their exotic cars with nice paint jobs, rims and hydraulics on them. It really looked like the average black neighborhood.

She pulled into the drive way of a two-story house and parked behind an all-white Range Rover, then they got out. Ameed simply followed suit. They led him up onto the porch, where he now saw that there were several young Asian men with sub machine guns standing around.

Kim spoke something to them in Chinese and what might have been the lieutenant, spoke back. Then they proceeded to the door. The outside of the house looked American but once he stepped inside, it was as if he'd stepped into China. There were statuettes, figurines and sculptures of various kinds in marble, bronze and even ivory. There were paintings and other kinds of art on all the walls.

Ameed kept his silence and followed as they led him to a backroom, where Kim knocked on the door and a command was given. She opened the door and he followed them both inside. The room was different from all others. In this room he saw several Asian women who wore lab coats and face masks. They were all working with what looked like the largest chemistry set in the world. He watched as one of these women in a lab coat suddenly looked up. She said something to a woman standing next to her then she started walking towards him, removing her face mask.

"You must be Ameed," the woman said.

"Uh, yeah. I was looking to meet with Mr. Blaze," he tried to explain.

As he did the woman smiled. "I'm sorry, Mr. Ameed..."

"No, not mister just Ameed. That's my first name."

"Oh," she corrected herself. "I'm sorry for the misunderstanding, Ameed. But Blaze is neither male nor female. Blaze is actually a branch of the Green Dragon Empire. If it were a representative of Blaze that you expected to meet, then that would be me. My name is Michelle Cho'."

"So, you're the person in charge?"

"Not necessarily. But I am the person you need to see. I believe you're looking to purchase some Ecstasy and maybe some of the marijuana they call Irene."

It surprised him to some degree to realize that he would be making a drug deal with a woman. "Yes. But I think what I need maybe a pretty big order."

Can you cover it?"

He tilted his head in thought. Out of all the money they'd moved around. Snipes had also given him and Pat five million of the remaining ten million. Which in turn left him and Kenya with five million. He'd told Ameed to have 500,000 put into Pat's name at a bank, which was later converted into a joint account. He'd pretty much done the same thing with Kenya. To buy the product he needed for this hustle, the money would have to come out of his pocket. Aside from the one million they'd each put in a safe deposit box at a Wells Fargo down on Pantherfavill Rd, they had the rest in the safe at the condo. So, his hustle would have to come out of that.

"About 25 grand for the pills and 25 grand for the Irene," he told her.

"My, that is a large order and how will you pay?"

"It'll be cash."

"Do you have a way to transport it and somewhere to hide it? Because once the air seal is broken on the Irene, it will smell very loudly. Unless it's re-air sealed," she explained.

"I have both. All I need to know is when to bring the money and pick up the product."

****

"I think we've got a hit," Special Agent Ashley Flowers said.

Drawing Chester Simkins, the agent in charge, away from what he'd been looking into. They were standing inside of the Federal Data base center, inside the Federal Bureau of Investigation at Ft. Lauderdale Florida.

"Show me what you've got," Special Agent in Charge, Simkins said as he came over.

Up on the wall screen was a 74-inch monitor that was used to display computer information and data. The screen was touch sensitive and Agent Flowers reached up and touched the screen in several places. The images shifted and changed before their eyes.

"This is the partial print that was recovered from the crime scene. This is a matching finger print. Only with this one, we have three finger prints in all," she explained.

"And?" Agent Simkins asked.

He looked down at his field partner of the past ten years. Ashley Flowers was 36 years old, white, unmarried and had no children. She was 5'7" and 123 pounds, very attractive, with a slim athletic build. In the ten years that they'd been partners, it had taken everything inside of him not to have sex with her and there had been times.

"Well, the prints just happen to have been inside of a police cruiser. I looked and the story is that the police arrested a youth in a car theft. They mistakenly placed the youth in the car without cuffs while they chased another youth that fled," she paused at every turn to be sure that he was following her. "The youth somehow kicked the section glass forward and climbed into the front seat. He then stole the car, taking the other police on a nice chase. In the end, the youth escaped. It looked like he tried to wipe the car for prints, but missed these three on the door."

Agent Simkins was feeling an erection coming. It was at times like this when he really became excited. "Okay, so let's hate it, who's the kid with the David Blaine in his blood?"

"Uh, well. That's the thing," Agent Flowers said. "This kid has never been finger printed, so there isn't a criminal file on him. There's no positive ID and the name that he gave the officers upon arrest, well, the name doesn't make sense."

Now Agent Simkins looked at her in confusion. "Wait a minute, how does the name not make sense?"

"Well, we ran the name through our data base and we did get a hit on it. A good hit," she said.

He felt his erection getting stronger. Agent Simkins was thinking that he might just give her the wood tonight. "Okay, then let's go get our man."

It had been almost a year later since the heist had gone down and it had taken that long just to get this hit.

"Okay, here's the funny part," she started. "Remember, you just called this guy David Blaine, how about Chris Angel? The name he gave the police was Ricardo Stokes, but the only Ricardo Stokes we know of isn't a youth. He's a 45-year-old convicted drug dealer, who, I might add, is currently serving a 180-month sentence at the Louisville Kentucky Federal Prison. He has exactly 24 months left on his sentence," she explained.

For a moment everything was silent. Not a word was spoken as the reality began to register.

"So," she picked up. "Either someone made up what they thought was a fictitious name. Which just happen to hit on someone who's a real criminal. Or, this youth knows this Ricardo Stokes from somewhere. A son, or nephew maybe. Could have been a kid in his old neighborhood, but it's something."

Yeah, but it doesn't add up, Agent Simkins thought to himself. How would a kid know about a heist of this level? And how did he manage to kill all of those people, then flee the scene with that much money? On top of all that, how in the hell, if he had the money that was taken, hadn't they heard a damn world about it? She'd said a youth. So, give or take a few years, this kid would be between 17 and 21. Agent Simkins simply refused to believe that a kid, with 88 million, didn't make any noise. That was impossible. Grown men with one million made noise. They bought expensive cars with loud music, big houses and drugs. They had girls and impressed their neighborhoods by throwing big parties that would be talked about for years.

A youth with 80 something million. Silent, making no noise. That just didn't make sense. Maybe they had been holding this kid as a hostage and killed him when they got away with the money. That would explain the print. Maybe.

****

Chief Investigator Bradly Wilson was also looking for the mysterious youth who was involved. Only he had a name and a description, yet he still couldn't believe that nothing came up. He'd put the names Merrick Stokes and Tiffany Stokes up throughout seven states and not one of them came up with anything. Not even anything on the little sister, Jennifer Stokes. He knew she had to be in school somewhere, unless she was being home schooled. But it just seemed that they fell off the face of the earth and he couldn't understand it. But, 88 million was a lot of money and with some brains, a family could definitely disappear. Which looked more like the case all the time.

Trai'Quan

122

CHAPTER FIFTEEN

Twenty-one-gun salute, dress in fatigue black jeans and boots, when I stepped upon the scene all I seen was troops... This lil nigga nas think he live like me, Talkin bout he left the hospital took five like me.... You livin fantasy's nigga, we reject your deposit...—Tupac—Against All Odds

Summer Madness

"Hold up. Is this nigga serious?" Zoe asked as he looked around the lounge at everyone present.

Merrick had just gotten his entire team together and made an announcement. Present at this meeting, was his moms, sister, Kenya, Ameed, Patrice, Tammy, her son Kevin, Gina with her two kids, Zoe and Lil mama with their three kids. Both JT and Hightower and Julius with Marion. His whole family.

"Did he just say what I think he said?" Tammy asked.

Merrick stood in front of them letting it soak in. Then he explained, "Listen, I'm serious. This is not a joke and truthfully speaking, you people know me, you know I don't play games like this." He looked at each of them. Then he continued, "So June seventh, a Caribbean cruise ship sets sail from Charleston SC. It's a two-week cruise and everyone in this room, with the exception of a few girlfriends, whom some haven't decided their taking yet and Marion's kids who aren't here, is included. All of you are being given an all-expense paid trip, all you've have to do is show up in three weeks with your bags."

Half the people in there had never even been on a boat, much less a cruise ship. They were all trying to imagine it, two whole weeks, going to the Caribbean Islands and back and they didn't have to spend a dime.

"But listen," Merrick put in. "For those who work for the M&A Corporation, when we get back, make sure you have that SS back at work. No complaints. Because also starting the 27th of June, we're opening a bails and bonding company. Those of us, myself, Ameed and Hightower, who've never been convicted of a crime. We're going to have to get certified to become bounty hunters, which means you women will pretty much be running the limo service by yourselves. I mean, we'll hire some more drivers, but most of you guys will be involved in this project." He paused, looking around the lounge at everyone. "Understand this, M&A Corporations has a goal, which is to make money, help black people who want to help themselves and most importantly, avoid the BS." He smiled at them. "So, enjoy the vacation, enjoy the cash bonus's I've given you and embrace Omerta to the fullest. Remember, that is our law!"

With that said, he ended the meeting and went to talk with Jen.

After he finished talking with Jen, he made his way over to find Julius, who he saw at the bar, looking like he was trying to mack on his moms.

"Ahem," he cleared his throat.

"Oh, Merrick, you need something?" His moms asked.

He looked from her to Julius. "Yeah, for you two to not do nothing I wouldn't do. There are some kids around." He laughed. "But seriously, I need to speak with Julius right quick."

"Oh, okay. I'll catch up with you later Julius."

He waited for her to leave before he spoke.

"What's on your mind, young man?" Julius asked.

"First off, I really don't mind you and my mom's kickin' it like y'all some teenagers, but that's my heart, bruh, so don't do nothing to break it," he warned.

Julius looked into Merrick's eyes and saw the seriousness. If he had learned one thing when Merrick came to ask him to move to Atlanta and become his advisor/mentor, it was that Merrick didn't play games. Everything with him was serious. "Yeah, I've got you," he responded. He really did like Tiffany and he didn't intend to do anything wrong where she was concerned anyway.

"A'ight. But on this other thing, am I good for this trip come Wednesday?" Merrick asked.

"As a matter of fact, swing by the office tomorrow and pick up the paperwork. With it, everything should be alright," Julius informed him.

****

"Mind if I have a word with you?" Kenya asked.

She'd just walked up to where Tammy was in the process of pouring herself another drink. Tammy looked up at the tall, dark skinned woman. She was only 5'10" herself and Kenya was known for wearing heels.

"Of course. What would you like to talk about?"

With her also being the oldest, Tammy was 28 and would be seeing her 29th birthday right after Merrick's 21st but she was curious as to why Merrick's girlfriend would pull up on her. It wasn't like she'd done anything with Merrick. As bad as she wanted to, she hadn't had sex since before she moved from Augusta. But she wasn't going to violate either, she owed Merrick too much. Her whole life had changed because of him and she wasn't about to start beefing with his girlfriend.

"It's about Merrick," Kenya said.

"What about him?" Tammy asked. Even as she asked the question, she hadn't been paying attention to the way that Kenya had been looking at her.

Kenya had asked Merrick a short time ago if there was anything between him and Tammy and he had told her that there wasn't. He had also explained their relationship and admitted that he found Tammy very attractive, which was something Kenya agreed with him on. Tammy was dark brown skinned and sort of favored a darker version of Laura London, with a few more curves. Tammy was a 33-24-38 and Kenya took note of her every curve in the Versace dress that she wore.

"He, uh. He explained to me how the relationship between the two of you is," Kenya began. "And he told me that there were times when he wanted to be with you."

"Uh, He told you that?" Tammy asked.

"We built our relationship upon two main concepts. The first is truth and the second is understanding. So, there are no secrets between me and Merrick," Kenya said.

Tammy was surprised. "Okay..., but I've never come on to Merrick. So, you don't have to think that I'll disrespect...,"

"I think you misunderstood what I was saying," Kenya cut her off. "Look, can I ask you a question without you being offended?"

"Yeah, I mean sure," Tammy said.

When the question came, both of her eyes opened wide at the same time.

"Have you ever been with a man and another woman before?" Kenya asked.

Tammy's whole way of thinking changed. She glanced around, saw Merrick talking to Julius and wondered if he had put Kenya up to this.

Kenya caught the look, too. "No, Merrick didn't put me up to this. In fact, he doesn't even know I'm having this conversation with you," Kenya stated sincerely, then sighed. "Look, the truth is, I've never done this before either. But when me and Merrick were first getting to know one another, he told me that before he cheated on his woman, he would share the other woman with her." She paused in her thought. "I personally think you're attractive and if this were to happen, I'd rather it be with a woman like you. But, it's just a thought. So, please, think about it. Who knows, we may even like it." Kenya smiled then she turned and walked away.

For the first time in her life, Tammy found herself checking another woman out and admiring her ass.

****

"Still nothing on the black kid?" Vincent asked. He was driving over into Staten Island to see some people about some business and when Bumpy called to check in, he kept telling himself at every call that this was the one.

"It doesn't seem like he has a clue boss. I've seen some of the reports from some of his people, but this kid seems to have vanished," Bumpy told him.

Vincent continued driving, thinking about the situation. There was just no way this kid could have gotten away with that much money. Not by himself, somebody had to be helping him. When he'd first sent Bumpy down there, that had been his first thought, that Bradly was trying to play him for a fool and that HE had been the one controlling the kid. But Bumpy said he hadn't seen a black kid around and he confirmed that Bradly was indeed looking for the kid.

"So, what do you want I should do boss?" Bumpy asked.

"Let's give it another week or two. Then we'll fall back," Vincent stated.

"So, I won't get the daughter? She's real pretty too boss and she's a pritzy bitch," Bumpy said.

"We'll see. Just hang around until I decide," Vincent instructed, thinking that the daughter was also his wife's niece. Could he let Bumpy do something to the girl?

****

"Stokes! Get dressed, Attorneys here to see you."

Ricardo Stokes looked up from where he sat. He was sitting at a table, playing a game of chess with an Old Five Percenter named Islord. He heard the officer call him over the loud speaker, but he wasn't expecting a visit.

"Gone handle yo business, young blood," Islord said.

Calling Ricardo young because he himself was 71 and had been in the Federal System for a little over 20 years now.

"Bastards probably trying to bring back those charges they dropped," Ricardo mumbled as he stood.

He casually walked to his room. Once inside, he removed his shorts and pulled on the state pants. He grabbed a state issued shirt, pulled it over his head and covered up the ripped muscles that were a direct result of working out hard.

For some reason, he glanced at the photo on his desk. The one showing Tiffany holding Jen in her arms and a young Merrick standing next to her. He'd never even met his daughter because she had been born after he'd been picked up by the Feds. With him facing the Rico law, he had distanced himself from a lot of people, friends, family and associates. He'd chosen to do the whole 180 months by himself but he was good.

Quiet Money

He had entered the prison with a little something, it wasn't a lot, but he'd been a hustler for real. Ricardo had taken what money he had and made it last him the 12 ½ years he'd been in. He had tucked all of the pain and emotions into his pocket so, if these bitches were trying to give him some more time, he was going to make it a real problem. Shit, he only had 2 more years to go before he could be back with his family. Then there was the rat.

As soon as he was shown into the conference room and the officer closed the door, Ricardo knew this guy wasn't his lawyer. The man sitting at the table was grown now but looked like his mother had just spit him out.

"Is it safe to talk in here?" He watched as the young nigga smiled and stood. He came around the table and before Ricardo knew it, he was hugging his son.

"Yeah, pop, lawyer client confidentially." Merrick released his father and stepped back. "Have a seat, we've got a lot to talk about."

Merrick moved back to his seat and Ricardo sat across from him. "Damn, so you're a lawyer now?"

"Nah. Actually, I own a percentage in the firm, but we'll get to that in a minute." Merrick pulled out the iPhone he had in his pocket. Then dialed a number.

"Hello."

"What's up, Jen? Were you at?" he asked, while looking at his old man.

"On my way to get my hair done. Why? What's up, Snipes?" Jen asked.

"I'm sitting across from our father right now and he would like to talk to you. Can you spare ten minutes?"

"Quit playin', Snipes."

"Jen, since when do I play?" he asked. Then he passed the phone across the table.

When Ricardo accepted the phone, he had tears in his eyes but he talked to his daughter for the first time ever.

When he finished his conversation with his daughter, he thanked Merrick and then listened to what his son had to say. "So, this lawyer, he's helped you get your game tight? Is there any chance of a problem with the crooked cop?" Ricardo asked.

Merrick had just taken thirty minutes to explain most of what had happen. He didn't give too many details, but enough to show his old man that he wasn't playing with GI Joe's any longer. "I've got some people looking into that now. I'm thinking that me and my mans gone have to get rid of the guy."

"And what about his connect?" His pops asked. "Listen. For this crack to be sending you on these types of jobs, he's got one of the two connections. Either it's a person in the Federal Government, or its Mafia related. Either way, removing him alone won't solve the problem," Ricardo explained.

Merrick thought about it, he had actually considered the Fed connect. But the possibility of a Mafia connection was another story. He made a mental note to have Luke and Laura look into that. "Okay, pops. Don't worry about it. But look, our time is about up and there are some things I need to give you." He reached down for his briefcase and put it onto the table in front of them. He opened it and pulled out a thick stack of papers. On the cover it said: *Ricardo Stokes vs Federal Courts.*

"That guard who just brought you in, you know him?" Merrick asked.

"Yeah, CO Daniels."

"Is he cool?" Merrick asked.

"Pish. That nigga's a super cop."

Merrick thought about it. Then, as his old man watched. He opened the papers to about the middle of the stack and Ricardo saw that the pages in the middle were hollow. He watched as Merrick took the iPhone and its charger and placed it inside. He also took out a roll of bills and put them inside then he closed it. He stood and went to knock on the door. CO Danials open the door and looked inside.

"Excuse me, officer. Could you step in here a second? I need a word with you."

Ricardo watched as CO Daniels stepped inside and kept a foot in the door way so that it wouldn't close and lock him in the room.

"Remember that thing I asked you about?" Merrick asked in a near whisper.

"Yeah, yeah," CO Daniels said. He looked at Ricardo.

"You were serious right?"

Ricardo watched as the whole play went down.

Merrick walked back to the table and picked up the transcript. He went back and handed it to the CO. "Walk him back to his block. Act like you've checked this and then pat him down. Send him back in. That's it, that's all I ask."

"And you gone give me five grand to do that?" Daniels asked.

He simply couldn't believe this lawyer was going to give him five grand to let him slip this old man a phone. He watched as the lawyer reached into his inside pocket and pulled out an envelope.

"Five grand and my card is inside if my client should happen to need anything. If you want to make a little extra money, call me," Merrick said. "I do all cash deals so there won't be a paper trail. You good with that?"

"Oh, hell yeah." C.O. Daniels hurried up and slipped the envelope under his shirt, into his waist.

Merrick turned back to his old man. "Both Jen and my number are in the memory. There will be some money put on your books too. Anything else you need just call me or Jen, we'll make it happen."

Ricardo stood up and shook his son's hand. He still couldn't believe that he'd helped create the man that stood before him. But sure enough, it was real.

****

When he got back to the cell black. CO Daniels made like he'd searched the transcript. Then he did a thorough pat down in front of the officer that was inside of the control booth. When he finished, he handed Ricardo that papers and told them to let him back in.

Ricardo wouldn't have believed it if he hadn't witnessed it himself. Not police ass CO Daniels. He knew that the other officers didn't suspect anything. When he stepped back onto the floor, old man Islord looked up from the current chess game he was playing with someone else.

"They tryin' to give you more time, bruh?"

"Fuck yeah. These bitches got me all fucked up, but my lawyer wants me to go over these transcripts again. We might be able to wiggle out," Ricardo said.

"Let me know if you need help," Islord said. Then he went back to his game while Ricardo slid into his room and put his flap up in the window.

He sat down on the bed and pulled the money and phone out. He counted the money. It was an even grand. Then he went into the phone and looked at the pictures of his daughter. He sat there on his bunk and he cried.

****

Merrick cried all the way back to the airport and even as he boarded the plane back to Atlanta. He wiped his eyes; it was the first time in his whole life that he'd ever been into his feelings like that. He also felt like something inside of him had changed, he hadn't experienced any headaches at all lately.

He pulled out his own iPhone and called Luke and Laura. He needed to find out who was really behind Bradly. Then he needed to tighten that ass up.

CHAPTER SIXTEEN

The ship set sail on June seventh, just as Merrick said it would. Everybody he had presented the trip to was on it. With it being such a large ship, not everyone was given rooms close together. Some were even on the other side of the ship. But for some strange reason, Merrick, Kenya, Tammy, her son Kevin, JT and a girl named Pumpkin were all on the same level, on the same side. Everyone else was spread out on either another level or on the other side.

The first day Merrick spent with Jen and Tammy's son. They explored the ship together, leaving Kenya and Tammy together. He didn't waste any time thinking about it, there was too much to see.

****

"See that?" Perry asked as he pointed to a dark sedan that was parked up the street from Bradly Wilsons house.

"You think that's the big Italian guy?" Julia asked.

They'd been watching Bradly for a few days now and while they knew that the large Italian muscle was dealing with Bradly, they hadn't known that he was also watching Bradly.

Perry went back to listening in on a phone conversation that Bradly was having. They had bugged the whole house and were now sitting outside in a dark van, which was parked in the driveway of an abandon house. There had been a *for sale* sign posted out in the front yard, but they removed it.

"He's talking to Vincent again," Perry said.

They now knew for certain that Bradly was connected to the Mafia. When they received the call from Merrick, telling them what to be on the lookout for, it had been just enough information to point them in the right direction. Now they knew that what Merrick said was on the money. Plus, they'd been able to figure out that these guys were searching for Merrick. The only thing was, they had the wrong name. They were looking for him because of something about some money being missing.

"How much money do you think Merrick took from them?" Perry asked.

"I don't know," Julia said. "But from the way we've been seeing him move. I'd guess it wasn't small change, especially if the Mob is looking for him."

Not that either one cared. They no longer had any love for the Caucasian white man. Both had joined the Nation under Min. Louis Farrakhan's leadership, having seen and experienced the blatant disrespect and disregard for black people by the government. Their war wasn't with the blacks who got over on whites, their war was with oppression and the oppressors.

****

"Nigga, I know you ain't all on a Caribbean cruise acting all hood and shit," Li'l Mama said to Zoe as she dressed to go join the other women up on the deck to sunbathe. Zoe was trippin' about her two-piece suit.

"Um, um. nah, fuck the hood. You ain't wearing that shit out there," Zoe stated.

Because the bottom part of it was nothing more than a thong and he wasn't trying to see every nigga on the ship sweating his girl.

"Boy, please, sit yo ass down somewhere," she said, then grabbed her towel and exited the room.

****

"So, we'll have to go through police training school for six weeks to become fully certified to carry weapons?" Ameed asked.

Merrick walked beside him as they headed to the deck. He'd just explained what he wanted them to start on when the cruise was over. "Actually," Merrick told him. "I won't be going out for it. I'll have my days full with school."

"You going back to school? Serious?" Ameed asked.

They rounded the corner and by passed the shuffle board area and some other games.

"I've got to get my paperwork for business management. Julius says for us to make this thing really grow someone would need the two-year education." Merrick was in the process of explaining just as they were about to walk past the pool and then they both just stopped and looked.

The pool was actually crowded and there were all types of people in it, especially whites. But that wasn't what stopped them, both Ameed and Merrick stood there and watched as Kenya, Tammy, Patrice, Gina and Li'l Mama were laying out by the pool sun bathing. All five of them were lying on their stomachs with their asses receiving major sun worship. The best part of the whole vision was that they were all wearing thong type bathing suits, so their asses were on perfect display.

"I wonder where that nigga Zoe at?" Ameed thought out loud as he looked at Lil mama's ass.

"Shit, probably at the bar," Merrick laughed.

Then he saw Kenya look back at him, almost as if she had felt his eyes. She didn't say anything, instead she went back to what she had going on.

****

Bradly peeped out of the curtain but he did it in a way that wouldn't let anyone realize he was looking. At first, when his daughter came and said there was a car outside her window and a big guy was sitting in it, he thought that she was seeing things. Until he went and looked for himself. What really got to him was the realization that it was Vincent's guy. The big, freakishly large Italian that looked like he might have some type of mental problems.

What Bradly couldn't figure out was why he'd parked outside of his daughter's window. Or was it that he didn't know which room was which? He knew that Vinnie sent him to watch and maybe to take care of Merrick once they found him. But now he was second guessing that, now he was wondering if Vincent was thinking about causing harm to him and his family. It wouldn't surprise him, he thought.

He watched the car for a few more minutes and it didn't seem as if this guy was going anywhere.

****

Bumpy sat behind the wheel with the street light shining on the car. He held an ink pen in one hand and a folded newspaper in the other. He was in the process of doing the Sudoku puzzle. He'd actually gotten better at doing them, especially when he didn't have anything else to do. At the moment, with all of the lights out in the house, there was nothing else better to do.

****

138

Agent Simkins looked over all of the paperwork before him and he still didn't see anything that stood out. What he was looking at was everything that they could dig up on Ricardo Stokes. The information dated as far back to when he was at the beginning of his career as a dope boy.

Ricardo's history read like a book itself and it all started when he was somewhere around 16 or 17. His very first brush with Law enforcement was when he had beaten some other guy up really bad. The other guy was two years older than him and was known as the neighborhood bully. Something happens to make them cross paths.

Ricardo's next arrest was when he was 18. He and another guy knocked over a liquor store. They got away with the robbery, but were later stopped by a patrol police officer and searched. Ricardo had the 357 on him. He got off with boot camp for the gun and no paper, but caught his next arrest three weeks out of boot camp. This one was simple, a public disturbance. He'd had an argument with some people in an apartment building and someone call the cops.

It was also at this point that someone made a side note in the report. It said, *"Suspect met Adrian Perez around this time."* This was also how he came to the attention of the FBI. It seemed they were already watching Perez and about to take him down when Perez brought Ricardo into the folds of the drug game. Over the next ten years, Perez would fall and his Lieutenant would rise, but at this point the FBI had an inside man.

Ricardo, having assumed control, also plunged in with the #1 drug supplier in NJ. A guy called Red Brick. Some simply called him Brick. This guy Brick, was almost big enough to be on the FBI's top ten most wanted list, because of his dealings with a South American drug cartel. Their informant, a guy by the name of Edward *Ed* Balding, was

Ricardo's best friend and had been working for the FBI since he'd first met Perez. When the power shifted, Balding attached himself to the next big thing, which happen to be Ricardo. With Blading's help, they were able to bring down not only Ricardo, but Red Brick as well. They also had enough information to indict a South American Drug Lord should he ever be caught upon US soil. With that bust, they'd also had to enlist Balding in the witness Protection program.

Agent Simkins went over a few more notes, then he pulled out his phone and dialed a number.

"Yeah," Agent Flowers answered.

"Book us a flight to Louisville, Kentucky. I think it's about time we had a sit down with this Ricardo Stokes guy," he told her then ended the call. Yeah maybe, just maybe they would learn something more face to face.

****

Merrick felt extra special. It was almost like being a kid and they told you that you could have anything you wanted from Toys R Us for free. When he walked into his room and found the lights dimmed with only three candles lighting the room. He looked at the two bodies upon the bed and heard Kenya say.

"Baby, just take a seat and watch. We'll tighten you up in a minute."

He suddenly realized who was in the bed with her. Kenya was lying back on the pillow and had her legs spread wide. Between her thighs was Tammy, crouched down with both of them naked. Tammy was in the process of pushing three of her fingers in and out of Kenya's very wet pussy. Kenya arched her back and pushed her pussy forward, allowing Tammy's fingers to sink deeper into her.

Merrick slid into the single chair that was in the room and got comfortable. He noticed Kenya trying to catch her breath and breathe easier but it seemed as if Tammy instinctively knew all of the right ways to stroke her fire. He watched as Tammy, still bending over on the bed, leaned forward and blew air onto Kenya's pussy. The position also allowed for him to look directly at Tammy's very pretty pussy.

As Kenya brought her head up, her eyes shifted between watching Tammy's mouth lower to her pussy and looking into Merrick's eyes. The whole sight itself was hypnotic. Tammy slid both of her hands under Kenya's ass and looking deep into her dark, blue black center, she brought her tongue out and took a lick. She'd somehow pulled a pillow under Kenya's ass.

Tammy was remembering everything that Kenya had done to her just minutes ago and she was trying to return the favor in kind, but this was a first-time experience for both of them. What made it even hotter was the fact that Merrick was sitting behind her, looking directly into her pussy, which was wet and spread wide before him.

As she sucked Kenya's pussy lips into her mouth, Tammy wondered who would be the first to feel Merrick's dick inside of them tonight. What she didn't know, because she'd been so focused on nursing Kenya's thick juicy clit, was that Kenya somehow had communicated to Merrick to remove his clothes. Tammy somehow spread Kenya's legs wider and then pushed her tongue harder and deeper into her pussy. Their position literally had Kenya lying back, with Tammy on her front. She was sort of laying on her belly, but had her thighs spread wide apart.

Then when she felt the bed dip a little and the head of his dick bump into her ass, Tammy almost cried. His hands slid across the cheeks of her ass and he raised her up just a little as she continued to enjoy Kenya's juices. Tammy's' heart dropped when he began to penetrate her pussy real slow. She gasped as he entered her. She'd never seen Merrick's dick but at that moment she wasn't sure if it was because no man had been inside of her body in over a year or what, but she felt a sense of fullness. It seemed like his dick actually went deep enough into her to touch her womb.

Merrick leaned forward and bit her ear. "Damn, you feel good. I've wanted to get inside of you since we first met."

"Uh, God," Tammy mumbled.

"And it won't be the last time either, baby," Kenya said.

Which was music to Tammy's ears. She enjoyed it immensely as Merrick began to withdraw, then push back into her, picking up speed with each stroke. She wondered if he was wearing a condom because she wasn't on the pill and she wasn't about to tell him to stop. The way she saw it. Whatever happened, just happened. So be it.

CHAPTER SEVENTEEN

Ain't no nigga like the one I got, No one can fuck you betta, sleeps around but he gives me a lot, keeps you in diamonds and leathers. Friends they tell me I should leave him alone, uh hu... Tell dem bitches to get a man of they own....— Jay-Z & Foxy Brown—Ain't no nigga 1996

Ricardo Stokes was trying to figure out what was going on when the CO came to his cell and told him that he had another visitor. He'd been trying to figure out how that could be. He knew that Merrick was still away on the cruise.

He got up and washed his face, brushed his teeth and then got dressed anyway. He'd learned that Merrick had so much going on that at this point in the game, he wouldn't be surprised by anything. Or, that's what he was thinking all the way down to the conference room.

CO Danials wasn't there today, this time it was a pretty little, white girl, named Hodges. He'd started to try her several times in the past, but thought the bitch might be racist. But racist or not, the li'l bitch was fine.

She nodded her head as she opened the door to let him step inside. The two people inside weren't anybody he knew. Ricardo stood there silently until the well-dressed black guy stood up and introduced himself.

"Mr. Stokes, my name is Special Agent in Charge, Chester Simkins and this is my partner, Agent Flowers. We would like to ask you a few questions if you don't mind," the agent said.

"Am I being charged with a crime? Or the suspect in a crime? Should I get a lawyer?" Ricardo asked.

Agent Simkins re-took his seat. "No, you're not being charged with anything and I don't see that you'll need a lawyer. But if at any point you decide that you want one, we'll stop our questioning and wait until your lawyer can be present."

"Yeah, considering my lawyers on vacation until the middle of the month," Ricardo said.

"Well, we could always come back, but like I've said, you're not being charged with anything."

Ricardo thought about that a moment. If he wasn't being charged with nothing, then this was some snitch shit.

"Listen, before we even get into this, let me tell you right now, I don't eat cheese. I quit eating lunch up in this bitch because the meat sandwiches got cheese on 'em. So, if you're thinking I'm gone rat on somebody, you can save it," he stated.

Agent Simkins laughed. He even turned to his partner and said, "Muthafucka, I like this guy already, he doesn't eat cheese. Did you catch onto that?"

"Yeah, I caught it," the woman said.

Then everyone fell quiet for a moment.

"I read your file," Agent Simkins said. "Had a big ass rat in it, too."

"Muthafucka, couldn't eat enough cheese to get full. I bet that bitch loves McDonalds," Ricardo said.

"Yeah, he probably do," Simkins replied. "You have any kids? Family you know, you get any visits up in here?"

The first question alerted Ricardo to something, this muthafucka just said he read his file. Then he should know that Ricardo didn't claim anybody. So, what was really going on here? "Nah, bruh, I been in this bitch twelve years, any kids I made were in the shower stall on my block."

Agent Simkins nodded. "Listen, a few years back we had a case where your name came up. But since we know you been in here, it's impossible that you could have been on the scene."

"Oh, yeah, what kind of case?" Ricardo asked.

Simkins hunched his shoulders. "Nothing major. A kid got popped with a stolen ride. When the police asked him his name, he said Ricardo Stokes," he explained and was watching closely to see if Ricardo would give something away. "You just said you didn't have any juniors. So that means you're still the only Ricardo Stokes in our data base."

"But that's funny," Ricardo said. "I mean, you guys are FBI, right? Since when do you investigate stolen cars?"

"We don't," Simkins said. "The same guy left his prints at the scene of another crime and the prints crossed matched."

Damn, Merrick. How the fuck he slip like that, Ricardo thought. "Well, it couldn't have been me. I sold crack, I didn't steal cars or nothing else," he told them.

They all sat quiet for a while.

"So, I hear your about to get out. What have you got left?" Simkins asked.

"About 19 ½ months. Then I'm free."

"You going back into business? I mean, you won't be able to get a job and unless you get some money from somewhere, you don't have a lot of options," Simkins laid out.

It was at that point he realized this was about the money Merrick had come into. But the funny thing was, they didn't seem to know who Merrick was.

****

"So, what do you think?" Agent Simkins asked.

They'd just gotten into their car after talking to Ricardo and were about to pull out of the parking lot.

"I'm not sure," Flowers said. "At one point, I almost thought he knew something, but then for some reason, the feeling faded. Maybe we need to come back later."

"Maybe," he said. Then started the car and pulled out.

****

"You've still got your grape ape watching my house. I'm beginning to feel like you don't trust me, Vinnie," Bradly said into his phone.

"I mean, do I have a reason not to trust you, Brad?" Vincent asked.

Bradly thought about it ever since the job had gone bad. The one thing Vincent should have brought up, never came up. He never asked why there were FBI agents dead in the warehouse. He never asked why they were even there and that alone told the story. Bradly knew Vincent was up to something. "Don't play games wit' me, Vinnie. I'm not some dumb smuck, I'm a fuckin cop."

"I know you're a fuckin' cop. You're a crooked fuckin' cop, too. So, have you done any crooked fuckin' cop shit lately Brad?" Vinnie asked.

"You know what Vinnie, go fuck yourself. You hear me, ten inches. A good, black dildo. Buy one, you fuckin' prick," Bradly stated.

"Nah, you idiot. You fuck yourself. Do you know who the fuck I am?" Vincent had raised his voice now. "You son of a bitch, I ought to. Hello? Hello?" Vincent held the phone away from his face and looked at it. "The son of a bitch hung up in my fuckin face. This fuckin' cockroach thinks I'm something to fuckin' play with."

Vinnie hung the phone up and then tried another number. There was no answer but he left a voice message for Bumpy to call him back ASAP. It was about time he taught Bradly a fuckin lesson. Yeah, just wait until Bumpy calls back.

But Bumpy wouldn't call back. In fact, the very next time he heard about Bumpy would be in the news, two days later. The police found a dead body in the trunk of a car that had been parked in the parking lot of the 401 jail. No one could remember how the car got there. All they knew was the cause of death came from one, 22 bullets to the back of the big guys neck. The only thing found in the car was an ink pen, an unfinished Sudoku puzzle and a half-eaten ham sandwich.

****

Merrick ended the call and fell back on the bed. Behind him both Kenya and Tammy were still asleep. The cruise would be over in two more days but Tammy had spent most of it with them. They had all talked about it and it seemed that everyone was in agreement. What started on the ship would become a normal thing once they got back home. He didn't have a problem with that, in fact, he was all in.

However, that wasn't what was on his mind at the moment. His pops had just told him about his visit with the FBI and how they had his finger prints at the scene of some crime. He knew which crime that was. What he didn't understand was how he had slipped like that. He still couldn't remember what he might have touched, but then, his old man said they didn't know who he was. They had only showed up on his door step because Merrick had once used his name in a stolen car case. Merrick remembered that night too. He should have burned that cop car, but there wasn't enough time. They'd had the helicopter up in the air and he was lucky he got away at all that night. He thought that he had wiped that muthafucka clean.

So now he was realizing that he had to tighten his game up. He definitely wasn't taking that shooting class now, but he made a mental note to speak with Julius. He needed to know if there was a way to make his print disappear from the Federal computer. With enough money, he assumed that anything was possible. He made another mental note to check into that the first chance he got.

****

Ameed turned his phone off and sat it down. He was glad that Pat wasn't the sneaky type, because this girl Princess was about to get him into trouble. She had been blowing up his phone the whole two weeks and he'd just now called her back. It wasn't even like she didn't know where he was, or that he was with his girl. What she had just told him was the problem. She said that she was pregnant and Ameed was trying to figure out how that was *his* problem, until she said he was the only one she had unprotected sex with. He could remember the countless times he'd shot his seed into her three holes and he didn't miss either. He'd thought that she was on the pill, but now he was realizing just how stupid he'd been. He should have asked her and not assumed.

How he was going to explain this shit to Pat, he didn't know. She was not going to be feeling that. Then again, he wondered if he could keep the shit from her. Would that even be a good idea?

****

"I might know someone that could help," Julius said. He'd listened to Merrick's problem and remembered a situation some time back. He'd met a doctor who did plastic surgery. This doctor had once told him that he could change any appearance on the human body except the eyes. Julius explained this to Merrick.

"You think he can do that for real?" Merrick asked.

"I mean, it won't be cheap, but I believe it's possible," Julius told him.

"Well, how long will it take for you to set that up?"

"This doctor works out of Hollywood, Ca. He works with a lot of the big-name stars. I'll call him as soon as we get back," Julius said.

Merrick breathed a sigh of relief because that was one problem he did not want. In this day and time, a black man could get picked up for anything. So, until he met with this doctor, he wasn't going feel safe.

****

Ricardo used his iPhone to look up information on the Federal Witness Protection Program and what it said was that over 17,000 people have been placed in it. It said that the witness's families were paid an average of $60,000 a year until they got jobs within their new communities. It also said that the US Marshals service helped them find housing, work and schools for their children. They were given a secured network of doctors and other professionals. They helped witnesses obtain new social security numbers, open bank accounts and even find a church or mosque to worship at. Ricardo read that after witnesses got established, contact with the government was only required once a year, unless there was a change, like them moving.

Ricardo sat back on his bed and re-read everything that Google had to say about it. The more he read, the more he wanted to find the rat. He wondered if his son had enough resources to find someone in Witness Protection. If he did, Ricardo simply couldn't see letting this bitch ass nigga live. In his eyes, that was what was wrong with the world now, too many bitch ass niggaz were being allowed to breathe the same air as real niggaz. By doing that, it made figuring out which one was which hard, if not impossible.

Ricardo knew he couldn't kill every rat in the world, but if he could kill this one, he knew that the world would be a better place. He logged off Google and then logged onto his Instagram. He'd just met this freak who liked to talk about weird shit, late at night. He was praying that she didn't turn out to be a fuck nigga because he would damn sure hunt that bitch down when he got out and kill him. Fuck niggaz ain't got no business trying to trick real niggaz on Social media. That was just some sick shit.

CHAPTER EIGHTEEN

Inside my lab, I'm going mad, I took two tokes of my blunt and started breaking down the flag. The blue is for the Crips the red is for the Bloods, the white is for the cops and the stars come from the clubs....— RZA— Wutang Forever 1996

The rat sat in the interview room. He was calm, even though he was in handcuffs, he really didn't feel like he had anything to worry about. He'd been picked up for having a large amount of dope on him but when they'd started asking questions he'd answered. No, he didn't need a lawyer and yes, he was speaking on his own free will. The questions had all started out about dope. They'd asked a lot of questions about the nigga Ready Black and he really couldn't stand Ready Black, but he didn't have any good info on him. Then they asked him about stolen cars and who was stealing them these days. All he knew of were some small time niggaz and he gave them their names.

Then one of them asked if he had heard of a booster named Merrick.

"Yeah, I know him. He runs with that Muslim kid they call Ameed, from up in Harnsburg," he informed them.

The DEA agent asked a few more questions, then excused himself. He said to hold up a minute because he needed to check into something, only it wasn't him that came back. Now the rat was facing another white guy, this one looking like he'd just left an army boot camp.

"You told my detective that you know a car thief called Merrick. What do you know about him?"

"Who? Snipes? Man, Snipes don't boost cars no more," the rat said. "Merrick got a job at Domino's but then after he got that nice ride, he up and disappeared. Him and every nigga that knew him."

"What do you mean by everyone who knew him?" The detective asked.

The rat cocked his head, thinking. "Shit, the Muslim nigga, Ameed disappeared. Him and his bitch. Some hoe named Patrice. Then TJ and Hightower disappeared from up Broad Street. The nigga, Zoe, and his bitch left River Glenn. Shit, everybody gone."

The detective thought over what he was hearing and a picture was starting to form inside his head. "You say there was a girl that lived in River Glenn? What was her name?"

"Shiiit. Everybody called her Li'l Mama, but her name is Stacy something. She used to work over at Churches on Laney Walker and 9th Street."

"A'ight and your name is what now?"

"I'm Anthony. They call me Ant G."

The detective already knew that Ant G was a GH and was from OS, but none of that was important. He was thinking that he may be able to track Merrick by the girl, Stacy. All he needed to do was pull her Section Eight information. If she had an apartment in River Glenn, then she more than likely had kids. If she had kids, they were registered in school, on Section Eight and most effectively, they were on her taxes.

Yeah, he thought, *I'll know where Merrick is within the week. And then...*

****

JULY 2009

The operation cost him $180,000 mostly because he was paying for the work and to be bumped ahead of the doctor's other clients. Merrick had flown out to Hollywood, Ca for a week and had both of his hands grafted. That was actually what the process consisted of. The doctor had basically taken his skin from both hands and flipped it upside down. Instead of trying to create new fingerprint patterns, he reversed the ones that were already there. When asked, he assured Merrick that they would not match any existing prints of his.

That was done during the third week of June. The bandages came off two weeks later and to more or less prove it himself, Merrick had Julius make a copy of his prints. He then took the prints to his investigator, Perry North. Perry had someone at the GBI building on Patherfrvill Rd. run the prints for him and true enough, the prints came up inconclusive. They didn't match anything in the Federal data base computers.

When that news came back, Merrick was able to breathe easier. But at the moment, he was headed to a meeting at Julius' office, which they'd said was urgent.

"He arrived in Atlanta today and he's staying at the Red Roster Hotel on Candler Road, right before you get to Gateway Apartments, room 23," Perry North read from his notepad as he stood facing Merrick.

"But how didn't he find out where I was?"

"The girl, Stacy Truth, or Li'l Mama," Perry said. "From what we were able to learn through our surveillance, some guy named Anthony Leggins, AKA Ant G, snitched on you. He told them that everyone who knew you disappeared about the same time that you did. Wilson went to her old job and got her full name, then he contacted the IRS, who in turn checked their records," Perry explained. "Long story short.

They told him she was the assistant manager at M&A limo services."

Merrick walked over to look out the window.

"Another thing," Perry added. "We now know that he had been working with a guy in Elizabeth, New Jersey named Vincent Mendoza, who has strong Mafia connections. Mendoza is married to Wilson's sister. We haven't had the chance to look into Mendoza yet, but you asked if he had mafia ties."

Merrick nodded his head. The fact that his ex's little brother was a rat, surprised him. He'd always thought that Ant G was a standup guy. A young, stupid nigga, but he would have never picked him for a rat. The fact that he was, placed him at number one on Merrick's list.

Since meeting his father again, he understood how he ended up in the Federal Prison, because of a rat. He was doing all that he could to track that rat down, too. As for now, he had to figure out what he was going to do about Bradly.

****

"Hey, wifey, what's up?" Tammy asked as she answered her iPhone.

She was in the process of driving a couple to dinner in her Lexus limo, so she had to use her Bluetooth to talk.

"Nothing, I just got home from school and decided to check in. How's my pussy?" Kenya asked.

Tammy glanced into the rearview and saw that her clients were hugged up. "Wet, real wet. Have you talked to Snipes?"

"Yeah, he said there's some business that he and Ameed needed to look into, so he might not get in tonight," Kenya explained to her.

"Well, Kevin wants to spend the night at Li'l Mama's with her two boys. How about I bring the Hennessy Black and you get the ice?" Tammy suggested.

"Sounds like a plan. I'll see ya when you get here."

They ended the call and Tammy continued driving. She was thinking that she needed to tell Kenya that she had missed her period and that she hadn't missed a period in over twelve years. She knew what that meant and Kenya was now two and a half months into her pregnancy. Which meant that she would be right behind her. She wasn't complaining because she was now Snipes' wifey #2 and that was real.

****

"So, when are you going to tell Pat?" Merrick asked.

At the moment Ameed was driving his new Ferrari Spider like he was a NASCAR driver, weaving in and out of traffic. Merrick had told them that since he'd had the operation, they could start to enjoy their money a little. Plus, it had now been over a year since that job and the bulk of the money was nowhere near touchable. So, the first thing Ameed did was buy a sports car.

He gave his Denali to Princess because she didn't have a dependable ride, plus she'd agreed to leave the club and the escort business. But there were two catches: First, Ameed had agreed to build her a full escort service under the M&A Corporation name, which would be run by her. She would own approximately 70% of it, with him and Merrick splitting the other 30%. She could hire any women she wanted and they could use the limo service as exclusive chauffeurs. They now had 4 new drivers. The second thing was, she wanted him to tell Patrice. She said that she wasn't going to hide it, nor was she trying to come between him and her.

"When we get this business taken care of, probably," Ameed told him as he drove.

Merrick had given him the rundown, so they were now on their way to the hotel. Merrick didn't see any logical reason to draw the meeting out. He pulled out the Tylenol three bottle.

"So, are we going to kill this fool?" Ameed asked.

Merrick looked over at him. He shook eight pills out into his hand. "Why would *we* do that? I thought that everybody understood, we're in this to make money, not to keep doing dirt." He popped the pills and chewed them.

"Yeah, but you still brought dude to the A," Ameed said.

Merrick knew who he was talking about. When they were growing up in Augusta, they had met this bum one day at the YMCA, on Milledgeville Rd. At the time they had been on foot and since they didn't have his weight set at that time, they went to the Y to work out. The bum had been going through some of the used clothes they were setting out and Merrick didn't know what made him do it, but that day it had been cold outside. He and Ameed were dressed for the weather. Over his sweater he wore a thick Dicky trench coat, which was all black and he had on a pair of good gloves. Ameed had watched as Merrick took off the coat and gloves and gave them to the bum.

That was when they were 17. From that point on, whenever Merrick saw Monk, he would give him what money he had on him that could be spared. Monk continued to wear the trench coat and the gloves religiously.

Before the cruise, Merrick had gone back to Augusta and found the old bum. Over the years he had learned a lot about

Monk. Like the fact that he smoked crack and that he was an ex-US Army Ranger, who had spent 30 years of his life in the military. Upon being discharged, when he lost a lung due to a shooting, the army didn't really do a lot for him so Monk turned to the streets. He would eventually turn to crack cocaine as an answer to his pain, but then one day a young kid gave him the coat off his back and his gloves, so Monk treated these gifts with respect. When the young nigga came back and talked to him, Monk told him about his pain, the pain he never shared with anyone else.

Merrick, before taking his people on the vacation, had made arrangements and with Monks agreement, he had placed Monk in the Atlanta Georgia Regional Hospital and paid for him to receive private treatment. Monk had stayed there for just nine days when he told Merrick that he was good now, that he had control over his demons.

Merrick then bought Monk a Range Rover Sport and got him a one-bedroom condo in the Heist. He'd taken him to South DeKalb Mall and bought him enough clothes for a year. While Monk had been in Regional, Julius had set up a bank account in his name with a $150,000 balance.

Now Monk was one of them and he worked for the M&A Corporation. But no one other than Merrick and Ameed knew what kind of work Monk did.

****

When the knock came at the door, Bradly assumed that it was room service or something. When he walked over to the door, he neglected to pick up the S&W model 29, .44 Caliber gun. Not expecting any conflict, he left the gun on the bed and walked barefooted over to open the door. When he saw Merrick standing there with a smile on his face, wearing what looked like a nice suit and with another brown skinned guy standing with him, Bradly didn't know how to react to the situation.

"How's it going, Bradly?" Merrick asked.

"Uh, Merrick, um, how did you know I was here?"

"Do you mind if we come in? Oh, and we come in peace, so you don't have to think anything crazy."

"Uh, sure." Bradly stepped aside and let them enter.

Once inside, Merrick glanced around the room. He made a note of the gun on the bed. "So, what brings you to the A?" He asked.

"What brings me to the A? Why, you Merrick, you and the money you stole from me. I want it back!" Bradly stressed. He fell silent as he looked into Merrick's face, seeing something he'd never seen before. Bradly thought that he was actually seeing a superior intelligence in those eyes. Before, he had thought that Merrick was a flunky, just another nothing ass nigger, trapped in the streets. Until now.

"I'm sorry, Brad. I was trying to rationalize the reality of what you were saying. So, let's be, uh, truthful. One, I never took anything from you. Two, you were never in possession of that money, you weren't the owner. Lastly, you tried to have me killed, Brad."

After talking with his old man when the FBI showed up, he had Julius look into the situation. He now knew that the hit team had been GBI agents.

Bradly sighed. "Look, Merrick, let's be realistic about this. The whole thing was my job, I brought you in on it and what do I have to show for it? Nothing. While you're up here in Atlanta living good, spending millions. What did I get out of it, huh?"

Merrick gave him a look of confusion. Something was wrong here and he was trying to understand it. "Brad, what part of *you tried to kill me* didn't register in your mind just then? Because the code of the street is, you drew first blood. Which means, you forfeit all claims." He paused to look into Bradly's eyes. "Brad, truthfully, I'm the reason you're breathing fresh air right now. I'm the reason your family is still a family. Because on some street shit, I should have killed you last year, but I didn't. Instead, I let sleeping dogs lay and now you're talking about what I have?"

The question hung in the air and Merrick could see that Bradly still wasn't seeing the whole picture before him.

"And your friend up in New Jersey, Vincent Mendoza, it's a wonder I haven't gone back home for a visit," Merrick told him. "I don't even know this fool, but his people tried to cross me too. So, I don't owe either of you shit!"

"How did you find out about Vinnie?" Bradly asked.

Merrick smiled. "Your brother in law? Come on, Brad. I'm a millionaire now. Listen to me, I have the power. I'm like Goku from off of Dragon Ball Z. I powered up." He looked Bradly over once again, then he turned and walked towards the door and paused. "Do you know what a super Sai yen is, Brad?"

"No, I don't."

"On the cartoon, whenever Goku reaches a certain level, he transforms and becomes an even greater warrior. Once that happens, then there's a problem. Go back to Augusta, Brad, enjoy the rest of your life. Enjoy your wife and hope to see your grand and great grandkids. But, Brad, if I ever see your devilish face again, if I hear your name, or if any of my people are bothered or harmed, Bradly, I'll show you how to turn a cartoon into a real movie. And I will win."

With that said, he and Ameed exited the room, leaving Bradly to deal with his own thoughts.

CHAPTER NINETEEN

It's 7:00 on the dot. I'm in my drop top, cruisin the street I got a real pretty, pretty little thing waiting for me. I pulled up, anticipated. Good love don't keep me waiting...—Usher— Nice & Slow

When he pulled into his driveway, it was actually a week later because he'd taken his vacation time just to go up to Atlanta. To make it look good, he didn't rush to get back home, instead, Bradly had taken the time to observe Merrick's set up. Using some of the connections he had with the GBI, he'd found out that M&A Corporations had more going on than your basic hood/street hustler, turned business man.

From what they reported, there was no illegal activity involved. It seemed that one of them came into some kind of inheritance and the money was what established the blue print for its structure. But Bradly wondered what he would really find if he dug deeper, maybe an off shore account and a few shell corporations that they couldn't find the real owner of. Either way, as he sat in his driveway thinking, he remembered Merrick's statement. That he had the power.

Bradly sighed, grabbed his briefcase off the passenger seat and opened the door to get out. He was contemplating an early retirement. Especially when street punks go from being low level criminals to established business men and from what his friend at the GBI told him, if this M&A Corporation was crooked, then who ever helped set it up was extremely smart. There were no big or even medium sized loop holes. Meaning they couldn't legally investigate them without just cause and they couldn't see a just cause. Bradly hadn't revealed the missing money angle, he was still trying to figure out how he could get some of that money himself.

All of the lights were out in the house, which seemed kind of strange, it being only 8:00. But then he remembered that tonight was a volleyball game night and his daughter, Kristy would be out until after 9:30. Using his key, he unlocked the door and let himself in. When he closed the door and turned around, the hairs on the back of his neck stood on end. Instinct instantly drew his hand towards his gun.

"There's no need for the weapon." The voice came from the deeper shadows of the room.

Bradly turned in the direction and focused his vision. He saw the figure sitting in a chair and he also saw that there was another one standing behind him.

"Besides, you'd only make this guy mad," Vincent said.

"I think I'll turn the light on anyway." Bradly reached under one of the laps and twisted.

When the light flooded the room, his eyes looked around to make sure there weren't any more people in there. When he was sure there wasn't, he looked back at Vincent and his bodyguard. The body guard had to be 6'3" but wasn't really big, he was just big enough.

"I see you've taken a trip," Vincent stated the obvious. "Did you learn anything interesting?"

Bradly looked hard at the older man. He would have expected the first thing to be questions about Bumpy. "No. Nothing interesting," he mumbled. Mostly because he wasn't trying to help Vincent. That chapter, he felt, was over.

"So," Vincent nodded. "How's the family?"

"Why don't you just cut the bullshit, Vinnie? Let's get straight to the issue at hand," Bradly told him.

Vincent looked directly into his eyes. "You fucked up, Bradly," Vincent said. "You fucked up and now I'm not exactly sure what I should do about it. Remember when I told you that the nigger would be a problem and you said that you trusted him? You said that, Bradly. Now look where we're at. My men are dead and a lot of your men are dead. The money is gone and this nigger seems to have disappeared. That was all a year ago, Bradly." He fell silent.

Bradly watched as Vincent reached into his inside jacket pocket. He withdrew a cigar, sniffed it and then he licked it before he pulled out a lighter and lit it.

Vincent looked through the smoke at him. "Now Bumpy turns up dead. They say it even looks like it was a professional hit. But I can't figure out who would hit Bumpy. Can you figure out who would hit Bumpy?" Vincent asked. He puffed on the cigar, releasing smoke in thick clouds.

Bradly put the briefcase down and walked over to the bar where he made himself a drink. He placed two cubes of ice in a glass and poured some D'Usse over it, then he turned to face both men. "You didn't come all the way down here to be sociable, Vinnie and I really don't see why all the extra talk."

Vincent smiled. "You're right. I didn't come to be social. Truth is, I'm not all that happy these days and it seems that you're the source of my unhappiness. But I have two choices," Vincent explained. "On one hand, I could have this guy break your neck and all of my frustrations and problems would go away. Capiesh? Or, we can find some other way to make up for that which went wrong."

Bradly tossed the drink back, he already suspected that whatever this deal was, he wasn't about to like the terms. It would probably keep him from pursuing this issue with Merrick. However, the alternative was much worse.

His bodyguard, who was also his driver, followed Vincent out to the car and opened the door for him. Once they were both back in the car, Vincent pulled out his iPhone and checked his messages. He saw that there was a call from Andretti. He pressed the phone icon and it dialed.

"Yeah," Andretti's voice came through.

"What's the matter?"

"Look, Vinnie, I'm still having trouble over at the Casino and if you're not going to help me run it right, then you can just sell me your share," Andretti bitched.

Vincent sat quietly. This wasn't the first time Andretti chose to suggest that Vinnie sell him his share in their casino. Since Vinnie had left New Jersey without telling him, Andretti was probably feeling like he was running the casino by himself.

"Slow your horses, Andy, I'm on a short business trip. In fact, I've just concluded the business. I'm on my way back, so just relax, I'll see you when I get there."

He ended the call and fell silent. Vincent was now thinking about the problem. He did have a real serious problem. Namely the fact that on his own end, he was ten million in debt. He actually owed more, since they couldn't find the money from that job. Vincent had counted on the money, but his problem wouldn't have been so bad had they still been penny pinching.

After the Miami thing went bad, Bradly hadn't been very helpful. They could have still been getting one or two bags from the Hartsfield/Jackson International Airport jobs, which were nearly the same deal, but smaller. It was mainly the big bills that the banks were removing in order to burn. The $500 bills and the $1000. On those deals, Vincent would only get 2.5 million a move, which had usually been good.

He was in deep with the Irish Mafia, who he'd been selling bills too. The Irish had some method where they would bleach the old money, then re-print them as $50 or $100 bills and put them back into circulation. Vincent had been working with them long enough that when their casino got in trouble financially, he'd borrowed ten million from them, but that was around the time the Miami deal had been on the table and when that went wrong, the Irish began to come around. They didn't know the deal went bad, but since Vincent had borrowed the ten million against the expected money, they were looking for the bills that they had bleached.

However, a whole year had come and gone and they were starting to get restless, which was why he had come to see Bradly. Vincent needed his GBI connections because he wanted to put together a job and this time, they intended to get more than three or four bags from Harts/Field and Jackson International. He had to give the Irish something to calm them.

****

"Ricardo Stokes, pack your property, you're being transported," the officer in the control booth called out into the dorm.

"Damn, young buck." Islord looked across the chess-board into Ricardo's face. "Must be going back on those new charges you told me about."

"Yeah, I think so," Ricardo stated, but he suspected that this transfer was a little more than that. A few weeks ago, he'd mentioned to Merrick that it would be good if he could get moved to a better prison, one closer to both of his kids. Merrick asked what he had in mind and he said that there were three Federal Prisons that were close. One in Florida, one in Alabama and one in Jessup, Georgia. Just last week Merrick text and told him to put in for a transfer. He said it wouldn't matter where he said to transfer too, all he had to do was put in for it and he had, just five days ago.

"Look here, old man. Come help me get my stuff."

Once they reached the room, Ricardo pulled out the dummy transcript and showed Islord what was in it. "Listen, Islord," Ricardo said. "I'm giving you this stuff, you don't owe me shit, but I appreciate the knowledge of self that you blessed me with."

Islord looked at the phone, charger and the three rolls of money. He'd known that Ricardo *AKA* Superior, had been hustling cigarettes and a little weed, but he'd never asked.

"Look. What you gone do if you need this stuff?" Islord asked, looking straight at him.

Ricardo laughed. "I'll be straight, old man. Trust me."

****

EDGEFIELD SOUTH CAROLINA

The federal prison in Edgefield was fairly new, it hadn't even been open ten years yet, so they still had a lot of luxuries. One of those being that the prison seemed to be ran mostly by women. Ricardo was surprised that nearly every officer he saw was female. Intake took him only an hour, since he'd been the only inmate to come in on this day. What surprised him was that he wasn't being sent to the lockdown unit to await a bed space. Instead, he was escorted straight to B 100 house, which, unlike anything he'd ever seen at Kentucky, B100 house seem to be the good dorm. There were only 50 men per house, each with one-man cells.

"What's your name inmate?" The female dorm officer asked.

"Stokes," he replied and then watched as she looked at her clipboard.

When she found his name, she looked up. "You're in room 16. It's on the top range, back there." She pointed in the direction he needed to go.

He grabbed his bags and went to find the room, which turned out to be a corner room. He went in and sat his bags on the floor. The room was slightly larger than the rooms at the last prison. He was deep in thought when someone knocked on his door.

"Yeah," he called out.

The door was pulled open by a brown skinned dude who looked like he was in his 20's. "What's up, cuz? You just got in?"

"Yeah. Came from Louisville, Kentucky joint."

"Okay, okay. So, what's up, you banging, cuz?"

"Nah, bruh, I'm a little too old for that shit. I'm righteous," Ricardo told the younger man.

"Muslim?"

"Nah, God body."

"Oh. Okay. Everybody fucks wit' the Gods. You've got what three or four of them in here. Hold up."

Ricardo shook his head. He really wasn't into the social scene like that, he had less than 18 months left and he could do that without any friends. Before that thought could really set in, there was another knock on the door.

"Yeah."

This time it was opened by a dark-skinned guy of average height and build. He had a low haircut and wore glasses. "Peace, God!"

"Peace, Allah! Who you be?" Ricardo asked.

"I be the God Everlasting Truth God Allah. And you?"

"Superior All-Powerful God Allah," Ricardo said.

They began speaking about their lessons and Everlasting gave him the basic run down on the prison. "Yo, ya need to call your people, the God Black Life got a phone. I can put you on."

"Yeah, so how much are they going for?" Ricardo asked

"Pissh. The high, high sun. These 85'ers want the whole stack for a flip and one point five or better for a touch screen. Right now, the Gods only got that one flip in our camp and there's six of us now, with you. But the Gods gone make sure you get time," Everlasting said.

Ricardo thought about it, he knew that he would need his own. "So how do I go about getting one?"

"Shit. If you can have the gold Western Union, I could pull the Blood dude who got 'em over, right now."

"Yeah, do that. As long as he ain't on the bullshit. I can have the money wired ASAP," Ricardo stated.

"Say no more, God. Let me go get him." Everlasting left.

****

"How long does it take him to get the phone?" Jennifer asked.

"Girl, I'm standing right here wit' you. How do I know?" Kenya said.

They were standing inside the Super Walmart, at the corner of Memorial Dr and Columbia Dr. Jen had just put the five grand on the wire for her father and was holding the Verizon pre-paid money card in her hand when he called and said he needed the money. It just so happened that she'd gone to the Doctor with Kenya when her phone rang.

"Hello?"

"What's up, baby girl?" Ricardo said.

"So, you got the phone. Here are the numbers for the phone card." She called them out.

"Got 'em, but look, I just got to this spot today, so tell your brother it's all good. I've put both of your names on my visitation list. I didn't put Tiffany down because she's got something going on," he explained. "I put Kenya on the list too. So, whenever y'all wanna come, it's all good."

"Okay. We'll probably come this weekend," Jen told him. "So, this is your number. Do you need anything else?"

"Nah, baby, I've still got a few grand on my books. All I needed was the phone, but listen, let me finish getting settled in. Call me back some time later. Love you," he said.

"Love you, too." Jen ended the call.

****

"Okay look, God, here's the situation," Ricardo looked at both Everlasting and King, who was another God he'd met. "Everlasting, you're in control of this touch and King you keep the flip. It's on both of you to keep the bills paid and to make sure the other Gods get some phone time every day. But yo', there shouldn't be any arguments or emotional shit about these. The first time the equality is questioned, I'ma take 'em and give everybody the same amount of time every day," he explained.

Ricardo was doing this so that they would all have something. To have something, they had to appreciate it.

CHAPTER TWENTY

As soon as he buys that wine, I just creep up from behind, and ask you what your interest are, who you be with. You gone be here for a while...—Biggie Smalls— Big Poppa

"I think we might have something," Agent Flowers stated as she walked into the office.

Agent Simkins looked up from the morning paper and cup of coffee he'd been enjoying. "What?"

"Remember that guy, Ricardo Stokes?" She sat on the corner of his desk as she spoke. "Well he just transferred to a Federal Prison in Edgefield, SC. It's a new prison."

"So?" Simkins said.

"Well. You remember he told us that he didn't have any kids?"

"He said that he knew of," he corrected her.

"Well, he must've just found out, he's placed two kids on his visitation list. A daughter who's 16, about to be 17 and the son is 21. He just had a birthday," she said.

Agent Simkins sat there a moment, trying to figure out how all of this was relevant. "I don't get it," he said.

"Well maybe this will help."

For the first time, he noticed she held a file folder in her hand, which she passed to him. Agent Simkins opened it, then flipped through the file. When he finished, he looked up. "Get us a flight to South Carolina."

She smiled. "Already done it."

Agent Simkins looked at the name again, Merrick Blacksun and the brief history on him, which also included him coming into a large amount of money on his 21st birthday. The question mark came up when the IRS's note said they couldn't trace the money. It just didn't add up.

****

"I appreciate you pulling those strings for me bruh," Merrick told Ameed as he, once again, rode shot gun in the Ferrari.

"Don't sweat it. Besides, Princess said you're like family, so it was a favor."

Ameed had found out that one of Princess' sponsors was the warden at the new Edgefield Federal Prison and when he mentioned it to Merrick it was like a blessing. Merrick told him to see if Princess could get the guy to transfer his old man closer to them, which didn't turn out to be that hard. All he had to do was call in a few favors himself.

"Have you spoken to your moms about moving?" Merrick asked.

"Yeah, but she's still stressing that hood shit. She says she doesn't intend to leave the hood," Ameed said.

"Yeah, but they got hoods up here too." Merrick wanted to pull as many of his family together as possible and he knew that it would make Ameed feel better to have his moms up in the A with them.

"Don't worry about it. But, yo, what do you think this meeting is about?"

"I dunno," Merrick said.

Julius had called and asked that they both meet with him but he didn't suggest what it could be about so they were now on their way to the office.

Ameed pulled into the parking lot and parked, then they both got out and went inside. When they stepped off the elevator and approached the office, Julius' secretary saw them and as they came up to her desk, she held a note pad up and they saw the message.

The FBI are inside.

Merrick simply nodded his head and they waited as she pressed the intercom.

"Mr. Howard, I have Mr. Blacksun and his brother out here to see you," she said.

"Please, send them both in," Julius said.

They opened the door and stepped inside. In the office, they found Julius seated behind his desk, looking as calm as ever while Marion stood gazing out one of the windows. Sitting in front of the desk, were two people they'd never seen before. Merrick remembered the description that his old man gave him, a well-dressed black man and a quiet, sexy looking, white woman. The woman held a brief case across her lap.

"Merrick, Ameed, I'd like you both to meet special agents Simkins and Flowers. They would like to ask you a few questions," Julius said.

Merrick watched as the guy stood and pushed his hand out, then cleared his throat.

"Ahem, I'm Agent Chester Simkins and you are?"

Agent Simkins held his hand out to Merrick, he knew that this was Ricardo's son as soon as he entered the office. The facial features weren't all there, but he did have the eyes. Ricardo, he'd known, had a mixture of Haitian and Dominican blood. When his name first came to them and he had gone over the file, those were two of the things that stuck out to him. When they'd sat down across from Ricardo in Louisville, Agent Simkins mentally told himself then, that he'd never seen anyone who was black that had predatorial grey eyes with light streaks of green and brown in them. Now he was looking into a set of predatorial grey eyes that were green and he felt himself getting an erection.

"Merrick. Merrick Blacksun," he said as he shook the hand.

As a curtesy, he introduced himself to Ameed too, but his focus was on Merrick.

"You look just like your father," Simkins said.

"Ha, that's funny," Merrick laughed. "Most people say that I look like my mother, but with my father's eyes."

Agent Simkins smiled. *Nice catch*, he thought.

"I stand corrected. Please, have a seat, I'd like to ask you a few questions." He turned to the woman. "Agent Flowers if you wouldn't mind."

He had instructed Agent Flowers to dress nice because it was a psychological tactic. He knew that most men, or most black men, couldn't resist looking at an attractive woman. Make it an attractive white woman, wearing an expensive Alexandre Birman suit, which fit her curves and Simkins wanted to see what this young man would do.

But Merrick didn't make it obvious, he instead moved to take the seat. Agent Simkins sat as well, while Agent Flowers stood next to the other guy and Ameed.

"When was the last time you saw your father?"

"This past weekend. My sister Jen and I, went to visit him," Merrick told him.

Information that Simkins already knew. When they reached the Federal Prison in Edgefield SC, they'd been specific about looking over the inmate's contacts. When he saw the names and that they had visited, he scratched their plan to talk to Ricardo. Instead they drove straight to Atlanta where Agent Flowers used her iPhone to Google the name Merrick Blacksun and M&A Corporation popped up. Along with it was a mention of the 15% ownership in Howard and Gibson Law firm, thus they arrived at the law office.

"So how is Ricardo? Is he doing well?" Simkins asked. He watched as Merrick sat back in his chair.

Not once did he look at the two lawyers, nor did he pay any attention to anyone else inside of the room. Instead he looked directly at Agent Simkins. "Why don't you ask me what you really want to ask? It seems you asked my old man something about a stolen car issue and some finger prints, which I think he said that also showed up at the scene of another crime," Merrick explained to him. "So, the fact that your now here, would suggest you are here about something other than my old man. So, let's not play games," he stated.

Agent Simkins held a straight face for a moment and then he laughed. When he laughed, even the female attorney looked back at him from the window.

"Muthafucka," Simkins said. He looked over at Julius and said, "I like this guy, nothing impresses me more than a man who's about his business."

"Yeah, but I thought your business was with me, not my lawyer," Merrick interjected.

Agent Simkins became half way serious again. "You know what you remind me of? There was an old TV movie that came out around the mid to late 90's. It was a Mario Puzd movie about a young Italian who moved up in the ranks and took power. I think the young guys name was Cross, but he eventually had these unique gifts for being able to out think everybody. You ever see that movie?"

"The Last Don. Yeah, I actually have it on DVD," Merrick said.

"So, tell me, Merrick, are you a Don?" Simkins asked, but he didn't wait for any answer. "Because we've looked into your businesses and while everything on the top of the water looks like water, we can't see beneath the surface. When the IRS can't see beneath the surface, do you know what that screams? Organized Crime." Agent Simkins looked into his eyes as he spoke. "And who does Organized Crime? The Mafia, but hey, this is the south, this is Atlanta. Other than a few black drug dealers, whom we hear about at times, who make stupid moves, we've never heard the name Merrick Blacksun. So, we checked and do you know what we found?"

Merrick was not impressed by this Denzel Washington, Training Day wanna be FBI agent. When he first met him, he thought that this guy was about to be a problem, even the trick with the pretty white girl that wasn't dressed like an FBI agent. When Luke and Laura came to his attention and he found out what they use to be, FBI and CIA, he'd made it a point to sit down with one of them every chance he got and ask questions. He'd listen while they both told him about Quantico, Virginia, which was HQ and paid close attention as they explained the inner workings of the two. So, he knew they played a lot of mind games.

"Why don't you tell me? I've got nothing else to do right now and I'm quite sure it's a good story," he said, then watched as Agent Simkins laughed again.

"Damn, I like this guy," Simkins said again. Then he became serious with his next words. "Merrick Blacksun don't look real. I mean everything's there, from the single black woman giving birth in Camden, NJ, the father not signing the birth certificate so she gives the child her last name, a name that seems to have begun with her. We can't figure that one out either." He paused to look at Merrick for a reaction, but there wasn't one. "There's school, no youth record, no crime. Which is damn near impossible for a black youth in Camden. Do you know that Camden, NJ is, or has been in the top five cities in the United States as the murder capitol? They were going neck and neck with Fort Work, TX for the number three spot for a while and you avoided all of that. Impressive." He shook his head in disbelief.

"My mom's saw it like that too," Merrick said. "But you're wrong, I did find interest in the streets. I've done my share of dirt, but unlike everybody else, my old man, who had real experience, told me when I was young that the real thrill wasn't in doing the dirt. The thrill was doing the dirt and not being caught dirty."

"Smart man." Agent Simkins looked up at Agent Flowers.

"I guess that's why he lied to us. Told us he didn't know he had a son."

"That he knew of," she corrected.

Merrick sighed. "Listen, I don't need you people to tell me who I am. I already know the story. So, let's stick to the script." He paused. "Why are you here?"

It was a simple and direct question.

"You see, right there, that's why the fuck I was talking about you. You're not an Italian, but you think and act just like an under Boss or maybe even one of the bosses," Simkins said.

Merrick wondered what he would think if he knew that his mother's family could be traced back to Corsica, Italy. Or his other secret.

"Have you ever been to Miami, Merrick?" Agent Simkins asked.

"A time or two. Why?"

"Do you know anything about Brinks Security?"

"You mean the armored car people? Yeah, I know who they are. What about them?" Merrick asked.

Agent Simkins fell short of words for a second. "A little over a year ago. Agent flowers and I were called in on a crime. It happened at the Miami International Airport, where a heist took place. I can't really go into the details and since we're not charging you with a crime, there's no need to alarm your attorneys."

"Well, then just what are you doing?" Marion spoke from where she stood. "Not charging, but accusing, is just the same," she pointed out.

Agent Simkins nodded. "True, but we're not accusing the young Don here of any crime. Are we Agent Flowers?"

"No, sir, we're not," she said.

"I was just telling Merrick about a crime. One where close to 100 million dollars was misappropriated and I was just going to ask if Merrick was anywhere near Miami at this time," he said all nice.

"I don't believe so," Merrick told him.

"There, see how easy that was?" Agent Simkins said. "Oh, there is one small request I'd like to make and it is a rather funny issue." He looked at both the lawyers. "Would it be possible to acquire fingerprints from your clients? Both of them?" He nodded to Ameed, too.

"Let me guess," Julius said. "If they don't give you the prints, you'll come back with a court order, right?"

They watched as Simkins held his hands up.

"It's okay Julius," Merrick said. "We'll comply."

"Great. Agent Flowers," Simkins said.

Agent Flowers placed the brief case on the desk and opened it. She then showed them what an electronic scanner was. "Just place one of your hands on the pad," she said.

Ameed stepped forward first. He placed his hand on the pad.

"The scanner reads your prints and using an FBI satellite uplink, it tells us if your prints are in our data base and if you're suspected of a crime," Agent Flowers explained.

"What if their prints come up in a crime you're not looking into?" Marion asked. "Then what?"

"Honestly," Simkins said. "We're only concerned with one crime. I wouldn't care if these two's prints came up in the disappearance of Jimmy Hoffa."

Agent Flowers looked up when Ameed's scan finished. "He's clean."

Merrick stood and moved over to place his hand on the scan pad. "So, does this stay in your data base? I've never been convicted of a crime," he said. "I'd hate to be picked up next week for something I forgot."

"It'll be in our data base, but local law enforcement doesn't have direct access to that, unless it's requested," Agent Flowers explained. She watched as the screen blinked as if there was a glitch, then it read: No Match Found.

"He's clean, too," she said, surprised.

"Are you sure?" Simkins asked and watched as she turned the screen to face him. "Well, it seems that I owe you an apology, Mr. Blacksun. Truth being what it is." Agent Simkins stood as Flowers began to repack the scanner. "I thought you were the one we were looking for. I'm sorry to have bothered you."

CHAPTER TWENTY-ONE

I form atomically like Socrates' philosophies, or hypothesis can't define how I be droppin these mockeries, lyrically preform armed robberies, flee with the lottery possibly they spotted me...— Wutang Clan Triumph 1997

November 2009

"Shit!" Ameed exclaimed.

Merrick watched as his partner rubbed his two hands together then brought them up to his lips and blew warm air into them.

"Bruh," Ameed said, trying to keep his teeth from chattering as he spoke. "Are you sure about this info."

Merrick pulled his trench coat tighter around him and turned to look at JT and Hightower. Both were standing back in the shadows, where they could hardly be seen. He couldn't quite tell if they were as cold as Ameed, but he had told Ameed just before they left that they wouldn't be sitting up in a comfortable SUV, watching this place. Not like the first job.

"It better be," Merrick said. "If not, then yo girl gone give me my money back."

He was talking about Princess. Who had somehow become a real close associate of Merrick's and had it not been for the fact that she was pregnant, Ameed would have sworn that they were fucking.

After the FBI agents left a few months ago and he'd checked through Perry North and his connections at the GBI, he knew that he and Ameed's prints were now in the FBI data base and they were clean. With that knowledge and having Perry and Julia watching Agent Simkins and Flowers, he had also learned that Bradly was back up to his old tricks.

They'd botched a heist at Hartsfield and Jackson International and now the FBI were on that trail. With the Miami Heist behind them, Merrick had revealed phase three of his plan. When Agent Simkins had brought up the movie, The Last Don and referenced it to Merrick, he couldn't have been any closer to the truth.

In October, Merrick had started their extortion and racketeering business, being that racketeering also consisted of shake downs as well as illegal business. What Merrick had come up with while talking to Princess was, there was, in Atlanta, a lot of legal businesses that were doing a lot of illegal business. So, with Julius and Marion's help, M&A Corporations established its own Insurance and Securities firm, which also included their bail bondsman division.

Using Princess' Escort Service by having her girls find out about their sponsors and if these wealthy business men were doing illegal business, they were able to target certain businesses. Their first job had been a food distribution warehouse, which was owned by an extremely wealthy white guy, who lived in Peach Tree City. It almost went sideways when the guy tried to act like he wasn't doing anything illegal and threatened to call the police, but then JT and Hightower high jacked a whole truck load of products that were illegal. The cost to the owner was well above 30 grand.

When Merrick showed up again and offered to sell it back to him for just eight thousand, the owner, seeing that he really couldn't report it because then the cops would learn of his illegal business, instead, agreed to pay M&A Corporations Insurance and Securities two thousand dollars a month.

Merrick blew out a breath of misty air and had to agree that it was cold out there, but they needed this deal. This one was a little more fruitful than the first one.

Just last week they'd gone to Goldburg Auto parts plus, in Smyrna. He'd asked the Jewish man who owned it, to do business with M&A Corporations. By the information Princess' gave him, Mr. Goldburg was buying stolen parts. He had a guy in Syracuse NY who was running a major car theft ring and they were chopping up stolen cars and shipping the parts to other underground stores and business.

At first, Merrick hadn't been interested in stolen cars or parts, until Princess gave him some more information and he saw that the business was dirtier than it seemed. Goldburg had once been suspected by the ATF of running drugs and guns up and down the East coast. It seemed that he'd had some political power and the case eventually faded into the background. The ATF, Merrick learned when he asked Julia French to check on it, had been told that if they made a move on Goldburg and were wrong, the law suit would consist of harassment and discrimination. It would cost them millions and since the information wasn't 100% sure, they let it go. But Julia French, using some of her sources, found out that there was some truth to it. That the DEA profess to have people, snitches, who did business with Goldburg and they confirmed that he was dealing cocaine, heroin and even meth.

Merrick brought his head up as the head lights of an approaching vehicle caught his attention. He didn't even speak as he glanced over at Ameed. The truck pulled up inside of the warehouse parking lot. The warehouse was actually in Kennesaw, just off I-75. Neither the driver of the truck nor the passenger, saw the men standing outside. There wasn't any reason to expect anything, they'd been driving the route for seven months now. When they first picked up the job, they were nervous.

The driver turned the truck and backed up to the warehouse loading docks and the passenger jumped out. He ran around back to make sure it was a good docking. Once he was sure the docking was good, the driver turned the truck off. Then they waited. As the minutes passed, he began to wonder about his partner. He should have been back by now; they were waiting for the Jewish guy's people to come unload the truck.

When he looked into the rearview, he saw that the warehouse door was partly lifted. *Shit. This fool must be being nosey*, he thought. He didn't want to get into any trouble for something stupid, so he opened his door and climb down out of the truck.

"Jack. We ain't supposed to be in these people's warehouse," he called out.

Then he heard a cough and turned to look behind him. He saw the two black guys walking towards him with baseball bats and then two more seemed to appear from out of the warehouse. The driver, seeing that this was about to be a problem, reached towards the .38 that was in his waist.

"Bad move, buddy," the guy in the black trench coat called out. The driver hesitated in mid-reach; he saw that the other guy with him already had a Taurus SP brand with the laser sight on top. The sight of the gun made him pause.

"Your friend, Jack, is alright. He's got a few broken ribs and may have a headache when he wakes up. If I were you, I wouldn't do anything stupid," Merrick said.

The driver watched in silence as the two with the bats moved up and took the gun from him. They passed it to the guy who was talking. The guy now holding the gun, used it to backhand the driver across the jaw. The driver stumbled and felt the warm wetness on his lips, he knew it was his own blood. As he straightened up, one of them used a bat and hit him solidly in his ribs. The driver heard the bones crack, then they both commence to beating him and nearly caused him to black out. When they stopped and stepped back, even with one eye nearly closed and a headache coming on, he could still see the black shoes in front of him.

"We're only taking the shipment," Merrick said. "Give Mr. Goldburg a message for me. Tell him the drugs are a lost cause. He won't get those back, but the parts and the guns he can have back, once he agrees to the terms I've set. Also, tell him that his drug trafficking days end here. Or else."

The driver then watched as the foot drew back and the guy kicked him hard in the side of the head. This time he did go out.

****

"Fuck!" David Goldburg Jr cursed.

He wasn't even thinking about his religious beliefs at the moment because he was emotionally disturbed.

"Mr. Goldburg, if you want, I think I can describe these guys to the cops.

"No!" David said. "No cops. I hate cops," he stated then looked across his desk to both Jack and Mel. "You two go home, I'll think of something."

He watched as they got up to leave. Then he thought about the message. David already knew who these guys were. The people from M&A and it was clear that they knew about the drugs and the guns. Well, they said the drugs were lost. He'd laughed at them when they came to see him. Now they'd high jacked a $2.5 million dollar shipment and were only offering to give him $1 million dollars' worth of it back.

He reached out to press the intercom button. "Carol, get me the number for M&A Insurance and Securities, will you? It's located somewhere in DeKalb. Yeah, yeah, I know we've got good insurance as it is, I just need to talk to these guys."

****

Merrick and Ameed both now had office space inside of the same building that housed the law firm, but the offices for M&A Corporations were on the seventh floor and at the end of the East Hall. There were two secretaries that sat at desks out front. Both of them were sisters from the Nation of Islam and while they didn't wear the large over garments like the Muslim women in the Middle East, they were respectfully dressed in women's business clothes and they still wore their head pieces.

Merrick was thinking about something Princess had just told him before she had left his office, not too long ago. The information was about a white guy who was part owner in Georgia's United Fire Arms and Dealerships, which was located in Stockbridge off I-675, but the guy lived in Fayetteville. Princess said one of her girls found out that this guy was moving guns out of an f-250 in some of the black projects. He had that on his table and it seemed that Bradly couldn't leave well enough alone, which was his thought as his intercom buzzed.

"What is it, Jalisa?"

"Mr. Blacksun, I have a Mr. Goldburg on the line. He says it's important that he speaks with you," she explained.

At her mention of Goldburg, he put Bradly's disrespects to the side for the moment. "Go ahead, put the call through." Then he heard the line click.

"Ah, Mr. Blacksun. It seems you left me a rather disturbing message and I must say, you're more organized then I expected. But, now that you've made your point, my employers would appreciate if you returned our merchandise at once. All of it, I might add."

Merrick couldn't suppress it, he tried to, but wasn't able to hold it in any longer, he laughed hard. "I'm sorry, you'll have to excuse me, but I think somewhere along the line I misheard you. You want me to return to you what you think is yours?"

"That would be correct," Goldburg said.

He laughed again. "No, seriously. I'm afraid you don't fully understand the situation Mr. Goldburg, I have nothing that belongs to you," Merrick said.

"I see. Well then, I'm afraid that some of the big players will have to be brought into the picture," Goldburg said.

"Oh, really?" Merrick asked.

"Please, stay close to your phone. You'll receive a call within the next hour and please, have a nice day, Mr. Blacksun."

Merrick sat there holding the phone and was trying to figure out what that had been about. This guy didn't even try to make a deal to get his shipment back and that was strange.

****

The mistake that was made, was or would be, the biggest mistake ever made. But at that moment in time, the people making it wouldn't know that.

It started with Kenya agreeing to go with Tammy to see the doctor. With her being two months behind Kenya in her pregnancy and their special relationship, Kenya readily agreed. So, they went to the doctor together. The doctor wanted to run some test to make sure that the baby was healthy and do a routine check-up on Tammy that was all.

****

While he waited for the call to come, Merrick's thoughts went back to the message he'd received from Bradly Wilson. A message that didn't make a whole lot of sense. It was a card that read, *'Christmas only comes once a year. You take from me and I return the favor.'*

It wasn't signed. But the only person he could think of to send him something like this was Bradly. Once again, he put it aside when his secretary told him that a Mr. Beats was on the line. When he answered, Mr. Beats ended up being an ATF agent and he wanted to know why Merrick was interfering in an ongoing AFT investigation.

****

They left the doctor and since they were in Kenya's Lexus RX300, Tammy asked her to swing by one of Kevin's friend's house to pick him up, which was over on Memorial Drive. Edgewood wasn't exactly a good neighborhood for Kevin to be hanging out in, but Tammy didn't want to tell him how to pick his friends. With Kevin in the truck and them leaving, Kenya decided to stop at Zaxby's to get something to eat and that's where the hit took place.

When she pulled into the parking lot, a black, four door, Chevy Blazer 2009 model, pulled up directly behind her

RX300. The Blazer was actually blocking her in. While Kenya had been looking for something in her pocket book, something else caused her to look up into her rearview.

"What the fuck?"

As soon as she said that and Tammy turned in her seat to look back, the three men who'd exited the Blazer, holding various guns from a Smith & Wesson M&P 15 semi-automatic to an AR-15 and another semi-automatic rifle, unloaded into the RX300 with everything they had.

The hit took place in exactly four minutes on the head. By the time people inside of Zaxby's realized what was really going on, only one woman inside saw anything and all that she could tell the police was the people who did it were white.

Merrick got the call an hour after it happened. He sat at his desk holding the phone to his ear, listening as they told him that both Kenya and Tammy, along with Kevin had been murdered. The headache came.

He dropped the phone and ran to Ameed's office. Together they raced down to Zaxby's but there was nothing that he could do. Not only had he just lost the two women that he loved, But the two seeds that were about to be born with his name, as well. His bloodline was lost.

Merrick's whole world shattered at that point and the ten Tylenol Threes he'd taken on the way, weren't helping. The headache he had now was beyond migraine, he could hardly think, it hurt so badly. Until he blacked out.

CHAPTER TWENTY-TWO

It's so hard, to say good bye to yesterday... –Boyz II Men

The funerals were all held on the same day and everyone who knew them came. Even Kenya's sister, Uniece and her boyfriend, Ready Black. Merrick couldn't even look her in the eyes, knowing that Kenya had been killed because of him. Nor could he tell her that, had he done something about Bradly then, her sister would be alive today. He couldn't explain that to anyone.

After the funeral he didn't feel like talking to anyone, so once the caskets were lowered into the ground and they began piling dirt on top of them, Merrick turned and walked off. He didn't know where he was going and the only thing that anyone saw, was an older guy in a black trench coat who had stood at the back, turn and follow him.

"Ayo, Ameed. Is he going to be alright?" JT asked.

Ameed looked in that direction. "Yeah. Monks with him."

But JT wanted to ask him just what the hell Monk did, because no one knew. Yet, he knew this wasn't the time nor the place to ask.

****

Bradly actually heard the news not long after it happen. As Chief Investigator, he would hear things like that. At first it was a triple homicide, nothing unusual, after all it was Atlanta and it was a black crime. So, he thought nothing of it, but then a few days later he sat in his own office and read the details in the papers.

The name Merrick Blacksun jumped out at him, so then he re-read the story again. This time it spoke to him in a different type of way. Bradly knew it was a hit and he knew who'd sent the hit team because he remembered, finally telling Vincent the black guy's name that they assumed had stolen the money. But he'd thought that Vincent had left the issue alone. Especially since they were once again stealing the big bills. Now this, Bradly wondered what the consequences and repercussions would be. Then he thought it was a good thing that he didn't have anything to do with it.

That night, when he got home from work, Bradly sat down at the table with his wife and daughter, Kristy, to enjoy a nice meal. His wife talked about her day, since she worked at the hospital, she always had something interesting to talk about. Then Kristy talked briefly about her day and then it was time for him to drop the bomb.

"I've decided to retire next year," he said.

"Are you serious?" His wife asked. She'd been asking him to retire for years, especially when the gang violence became so bad that it seemed they would be a threat to the police.

"Yeah, I'ma do it after the New Year. Probably start up an investigation firm. Maybe," he said.

For the rest of the night they made plans based upon that one decision. He'd just changed their lives and it seemed to be for the better. Later that night, as he was falling asleep, Bradly could have sworn he smelled something funny, but he couldn't put his finger on it and then he fell into a deep sleep.

4:13 AM

Bradly was awakened by the cold water that was tossed into his face. He felt like he was drowning, but as he tried to fight for air, he became aware of the fact that he couldn't move and then as his mind started to focus, reality started to set in. Bradly realized that he was sitting up in a chair at the kitchen table, but his feet were taped to the legs of the chair and his arms were taped to the arms. There was tape pinning his arms to the sides of his body and a strip of tape across his mouth. When his eyes focused, he saw that his wife was also taped to a chair across from him and to his right was his daughter.

Bradly looked up at the dark-skinned guy who had tossed the water in his face and he realized that he'd never seen this guy before.

"Right now, you're probably wondering how we got into your house without the dog barking out back, or the house alarm not going off," the voice said.

While he could hear the voice, Bradly couldn't see the person and he knew who the person was, he knew that voice.

"Maybe you should have checked on that bitch when you first came home, but you didn't. Had you looked, you would have seen that she was already dead," the voice said.

Bradly could see the panic in his wife's eyes and the tears that were falling from his daughters.

"You see that guy standing to your left? That's Monk, he doesn't do a whole lot of talking. He's more of a man of action."

Bradly looked at Monk and he didn't like the look of him, not one bit.

"You're probably thinking, these guys are not crazy enough to kill a cop and his family. That it would be stupid and the FBI would come in. Yada, yada, yada..."

He was thinking just that.

"As luck would have it, before you killed my girls, I came into possession of a large shipment of Heroin, PCP and some crystal meth, which has all been planted in your basement. You'll look like the dirty filthy piece of shit you are."

Bradly made an attempt to speak. He was trying to tell him something.

"What? Damn, I can't hear you with that tape on your mouth. Monk, how about you remove some of it?" Monk snatched the tape off as Bradly screamed. "You ain't got time for pain. Crooked cop, so what were you trying to tell me?" Merrick asked.

"I—I didn't do it. That wasn't my hit," Bradly choked out. "Listen to me, a few months ago, me and Vinnie got back into the money thing, where they burn the big bills. Well, Vinnie's in debt with the Irish mafia, he was selling the old bills to them and they were washing them, then reprinting them as $50 and $100 bills. That was the move," Bradly explained.

At this point, Merrick stepped forward out of the shadows and stood at the edge of the table, not far from the daughter. Bradly saw the S&W Glock 9mm in his hand. "Keep going, I'm listening."

He watched as Bradly swallowed the lump in his throat. "Vinnie owns a percentage in this casino. It's in Atlantic City and it's called Twilight. Well, he was fucking up the money on his end and he went to the Irish to get a loan. They gave him ten million. Vinnie didn't want the other family to find out, his partner in the casino is a guy named Andretti Luiz. So, he got greedy, hell, I got greedy. That's how the Miami thing went bad," Bradly explained.

As he talked, he was aware of both his wife and his daughter's eyes on him. They were also listening to the story, but he had to tell it, if he had any hopes of saving them.

"Vinnie doesn't like blacks. He hates black people all together. It's a passion in him."

Merrick was already thinking about Vinnie and making plans to deal with him as he listened.

"Vinnie was mad when the Miami thing went wrong, he was even going to kill me. But as time went by, he blamed the nigger who got away. He said it was because I used you that the shit went bad." He paused a second. "We were talking just before we tried the last thing at Hartsfield and Jackson International Airport. We were talking and Vinnie says, *Whatever happened to that nigger you had, the one who stole my money?* And I tell him I don't know. So, he says, what was his name again and I say Merrick, Merrick Blacksun. But I'm thinking, he won't be able to find you, shit, I couldn't find you by your name."

He fell silent and Merrick was able to put the rest of the story together. "Except, when you looked for me," he said. "You weren't looking for Merrick Blacksun, you were looking for Merrick Blackmon. So, you told Vinnie who I am now."

"It was a slip up, I swear. I didn't know his search would go straight to you." Bradly dropped his head for a moment. Then he looked back up into Merrick's eyes. "Please. Merrick, not my family."

Merrick smiled as he pulled out the silencer and screwed it onto his gun.

"And why not? Shit, you and your friend just took my family from me," Merrick told him. "Both of those girls were pregnant with my seeds and they all died." He walked over and placed the gun to the daughter's head and squeezed the trigger. "An eye for an eye, right? My seed for your seed."

"Oh, God. Kristy!" Bradly cried as he watched her head fall forward onto her chest.

Then Merrick turned to the wife who turned away from him. He brought the gun up and squeezed. "My baby's mother, for your baby's mother," Merrick said.

Bradly watched as the life left her body as well and there was nothing else that he could do. When Merrick approached him and raised the gun, he spoke. "Just do me one favor. That's all I ask."

"Damn, Brad, I'm really running low on favors. I mean, fuck. It depends. What's the favor?"

Bradly looked at his daughter, then his wife. He brought his eyes up to look into Merrick's face. "When you kill that devil, Vincent, could you please tell him that I sent you?"

Merrick thought about it. "You know what, Brad? You better be glad that I'm such a good guy. I'ma do that for you, I promise." Then he squeezed the trigger.

To Be Continued...
Quiet Money 2
Coming Soon

Submission Guideline

Submit the first three chapters of your completed manuscript to ldpsubmissions@gmail.com, subject line: Your book's title. The manuscript must be in a .doc file and sent as an attachment. Document should be in Times New Roman, double spaced and in size 12 font. Also, provide your synopsis and full contact information. If sending multiple submissions, they must each be in a separate email.

Have a story but no way to send it electronically? You can still submit to LDP/Ca$h Presents. Send in the first three chapters, written or typed, of your completed manuscript to:

LDP: Submissions Dept
Po Box 870494
Mesquite, Tx 75187

DO NOT send original manuscript. Must be a duplicate.

Provide your synopsis and a cover letter containing your full contact information.

Thanks for considering LDP and Ca$h Presents.

Coming Soon from Lock Down Publications/Ca$h Presents

BOW DOWN TO MY GANGSTA

By **Ca$h**

TORN BETWEEN TWO

By **Coffee**

THE STREETS STAINED MY SOUL **II**

By **Marcellus Allen**

BLOOD OF A BOSS **VI**

SHADOWS OF THE GAME II

By **Askari**

LOYAL TO THE GAME **IV**

By **T.J. & Jelissa**

A DOPEBOY'S PRAYER **II**

By **Eddie "Wolf" Lee**

IF LOVING YOU IS WRONG... **III**

By **Jelissa**

TRUE SAVAGE **VII**

MIDNIGHT CARTEL III

DOPE BOY MAGIC III

By **Chris Green**

BLAST FOR ME **III**

DUFFLE BAG CARTEL **IV**

A SAVAGE DOPEBOY III

By **Ghost**

A HUSTLER'S DECEIT III

KILL ZONE **II**

BAE BELONGS TO ME III

SOUL OF A MONSTER III

By **Aryanna**

THE COST OF LOYALTY **III**

By **Kweli**

CHAINED TO THE STREETS II

By **J-Blunt**

KING OF NEW YORK V

COKE KINGS IV

BORN HEARTLESS IV

By **T.J. Edwards**

GORILLAZ IN THE BAY V

De'Kari

THE STREETS ARE CALLING II

Duquie Wilson

KINGPIN KILLAZ IV

STREET KINGS III

PAID IN BLOOD III

CARTEL KILLAZ IV

Hood Rich

SINS OF A HUSTLA II

ASAD

TRIGGADALE III

Elijah R. Freeman

KINGZ OF THE GAME V

Playa Ray

SLAUGHTER GANG IV

RUTHLESS HEART III

By Willie Slaughter

THE HEART OF A SAVAGE II

By Jibril Williams

FUK SHYT II

By Blakk Diamond

THE DOPEMAN'S BODYGAURD II

By Tranay Adams

TRAP GOD II

By Troublesome

YAYO III

A SHOOTER'S AMBITION II

By S. Allen

GHOST MOB

Stilloan Robinson

KINGPIN DREAMS II

By Paper Boi Rari

CREAM

By Yolanda Moore

SON OF A DOPE FIEND II

By Renta

FOREVER GANGSTA II

By Adrian Dulan

LOYALTY AIN'T PROMISED II

By Keith Williams

THE PRICE YOU PAY FOR LOVE II

By Destiny Skai

THE LIFE OF A HOOD STAR

By Rashia Wilson

TOE TAGZ III

By Ah'Million

CONFESSIONS OF A GANGSTA II

By Nicholas Lock

PAID IN KARMA II

By **Meesha**

I'M NOTHING WITHOUT HIS LOVE II

By Monet Dragun

CAUGHT UP IN THE LIFE II

By Robert Baptiste

NEW TO THE GAME II

By **Malik D. Rice**

Life of a Savage II

By **Romell Tukes**

Quiet Money II

By **Trai'Quan**

<u>Available Now</u>

RESTRAINING ORDER **I & II**

By **CA$H & Coffee**

LOVE KNOWS NO BOUNDARIES **I II & III**

By **Coffee**

RAISED AS A GOON I, II, III & IV

BRED BY THE SLUMS I, II, III

BLAST FOR ME I & II

ROTTEN TO THE CORE I II III

A BRONX TALE I, II, III

DUFFEL BAG CARTEL I II III

HEARTLESS GOON I II III IV

A SAVAGE DOPEBOY I II

HEARTLESS GOON I II III

DRUG LORDS I II III

By **Ghost**

LAY IT DOWN **I & II**

LAST OF A DYING BREED

BLOOD STAINS OF A SHOTTA I & II III

By **Jamaica**

LOYAL TO THE GAME I II III

LIFE OF SIN I, II III

By **TJ & Jelissa**

BLOODY COMMAS I & II

SKI MASK CARTEL I II & III

KING OF NEW YORK I II,III IV

RISE TO POWER I II III

COKE KINGS I II III

BORN HEARTLESS I II III

By **T.J. Edwards**

IF LOVING HIM IS WRONG…I & II

LOVE ME EVEN WHEN IT HURTS I II III

By **Jelissa**

WHEN THE STREETS CLAP BACK I & II III

By **Jibril Williams**

A DISTINGUISHED THUG STOLE MY HEART I II & III

LOVE SHOULDN'T HURT I II III IV

RENEGADE BOYS I II III IV

PAID IN KARMA

By **Meesha**

A GANGSTER'S CODE I &, II III

A GANGSTER'S SYN I II III

THE SAVAGE LIFE I II III

CHAINED TO THE STREETS

By J-Blunt

PUSH IT TO THE LIMIT

By **Bre' Hayes**

BLOOD OF A BOSS **I, II, III, IV, V**

SHADOWS OF THE GAME

By **Askari**

THE STREETS BLEED MURDER **I, II & III**

THE HEART OF A GANGSTA I II& III

By **Jerry Jackson**

CUM FOR ME I II III IV V

An **LDP Erotica Collaboration**

BRIDE OF A HUSTLA **I II & II**

THE FETTI GIRLS **I, II& III**

CORRUPTED BY A GANGSTA I, II III, IV

BLINDED BY HIS LOVE

THE PRICE YOU PAY FOR LOVE

By **Destiny Skai**
WHEN A GOOD GIRL GOES BAD
By **Adrienne**
THE COST OF LOYALTY I II
By Kweli
A GANGSTER'S REVENGE **I II III & IV**
THE BOSS MAN'S DAUGHTERS I II III IV V
A SAVAGE LOVE **I & II**
BAE BELONGS TO ME I II
A HUSTLER'S DECEIT I, II, III
WHAT BAD BITCHES DO I, II, III
SOUL OF A MONSTER I II
KILL ZONE
By **Aryanna**
A KINGPIN'S AMBITON
A KINGPIN'S AMBITION **II**
I MURDER FOR THE DOUGH
By **Ambitious**
TRUE SAVAGE I II III IV V VI
DOPE BOY MAGIC I, II
MIDNIGHT CARTEL I II
By **Chris Green**
A DOPEBOY'S PRAYER
By **Eddie "Wolf" Lee**
THE KING CARTEL **I, II & III**
By **Frank Gresham**
THESE NIGGAS AIN'T LOYAL **I, II & III**

By **Nikki Tee**

GANGSTA SHYT **I II &III**

By **CATO**

THE ULTIMATE BETRAYAL

By **Phoenix**

BOSS'N UP **I , II & III**

By **Royal Nicole**

I LOVE YOU TO DEATH

By Destiny J

I RIDE FOR MY HITTA

I STILL RIDE FOR MY HITTA

By **Misty Holt**

LOVE & CHASIN' PAPER

By **Qay Crockett**

TO DIE IN VAIN

SINS OF A HUSTLA

By **ASAD**

BROOKLYN HUSTLAZ

By **Boogsy Morina**

BROOKLYN ON LOCK I & II

By **Sonovia**

GANGSTA CITY

By **Teddy Duke**

A DRUG KING AND HIS DIAMOND I & II III

A DOPEMAN'S RICHES

HER MAN, MINE'S TOO I, II

CASH MONEY HO'S

By Nicole Goosby

TRAPHOUSE KING **I II & III**

KINGPIN KILLAZ I II III

STREET KINGS I II

PAID IN BLOOD **I II**

CARTEL KILLAZ I II III

By **Hood Rich**

LIPSTICK KILLAH **I, II, III**

CRIME OF PASSION I II & III

By **Mimi**

STEADY MOBBN' **I, II, III**

THE STREETS STAINED MY SOUL

By **Marcellus Allen**

WHO SHOT YA **I, II, III**

SON OF A DOPE FIEND

Renta

GORILLAZ IN THE BAY **I II III IV**

DE'KARI

TRIGGADALE I II

Elijah R. Freeman

GOD BLESS THE TRAPPERS I, II, III

THESE SCANDALOUS STREETS I, II, III

FEAR MY GANGSTA I, II, III

THESE STREETS DON'T LOVE NOBODY I, II

BURY ME A G I, II, III, IV, V

A GANGSTA'S EMPIRE I, II, III, IV

THE DOPEMAN'S BODYGAURD

Tranay Adams

THE STREETS ARE CALLING

Duquie Wilson

MARRIED TO A BOSS... I II III

By Destiny Skai & Chris Green

KINGZ OF THE GAME I II III IV

Playa Ray

SLAUGHTER GANG I II III

RUTHLESS HEART I II

By Willie Slaughter

THE HEART OF A SAVAGE

By Jibril Williams

FUK SHYT

By Blakk Diamond

DON'T F#CK WITH MY HEART I II

By Linnea

ADDICTED TO THE DRAMA I II III

By Jamila

YAYO I II

A SHOOTER'S AMBITION

By S. Allen

TRAP GOD

By Troublesome

FOREVER GANGSTA

By Adrian Dulan

TOE TAGZ I II

By Ah'Million

KINGPIN DREAMS

By Paper Boi Rari

CONFESSIONS OF A GANGSTA

By Nicholas Lock

I'M NOTHING WITHOUT HIS LOVE

By Monet Dragun

CAUGHT UP IN THE LIFE

By Robert Baptiste

NEW TO THE GAME

By **Malik D. Rice**

Life of a Savage

By **Romell Tukes**

LOYALTY AIN'T PROMISED

By Keith Williams

Quiet Money

By **Trai'Quan**

BOOKS BY LDP'S CEO, CA$H

TRUST IN NO MAN

TRUST IN NO MAN 2

TRUST IN NO MAN 3

BONDED BY BLOOD

SHORTY GOT A THUG

THUGS CRY

THUGS CRY 2

THUGS CRY 3

TRUST NO BITCH

TRUST NO BITCH 2

TRUST NO BITCH 3

TIL MY CASKET DROPS

RESTRAINING ORDER

RESTRAINING ORDER 2

IN LOVE WITH A CONVICT

Coming Soon

BONDED BY BLOOD 2

BOW DOWN TO MY GANGSTA

www.ingramcontent.com/pod-product-compliance
Lightning Source LLC
Chambersburg PA
CBHW070501260626
47161CB00004B/1398